Susanna Shakespeare

Alida C. Rijnders

# SUSANNA SHAKESPEARE

Shakespeare's Daughter and Doctor John Hall

Publishing House ASPEKT

**Susanna Shakespeare**

© 2014 Publishing House ASPEKT
© Alida C. Rijnders - www.alidarijnders.nl

Amersfoortsestraat 27, 3769 AD Soesterberg, Nederland
info@uitgeverijaspekt.nl - http://www.uitgeverijaspekt.nl

Original title (2013): Susanna Shakespeare, Shakespeare's dochter en dokter John Hall
Author: Alida C. Rijnders
Translation in English: Alida C. Rijnders / Anna George, Bristol
Photograph of the author: Shira Koopman
Cover: Marieke de Beurs-Brommersma, using images from the Rijksmuseum, Amsterdam
Rijksmuseum Amsterdam: Aesculapius' staff, by Pieter Tanjé. / Portrait of Jacoba Vetter, by C.H. Hodges. / Portrait of William Shakespeare, on the title page of the First Folio, by M. Droeshout. /
Still Life with Flowers, by G.J.J. Van Os.
Appendix A & B and photograph Hall's Croft: Marieke de Beurs-Brommersma. (Appendix B after map from Fripp 1928.)
Interlining: Maarten Bakker

ISBN: 9789461536075
NUR: 321

All rights reserved. No part of these pages, either text or image may be used for any purpose other than personal use. Therefore, reproduction, modification, storage in a retrieval system or retransmission, in any form or by any means, electronic, mechanical or otherwise, for reasons other than personal use, is strictly prohibited without prior written permission.

*For Paul
and our family,
with love*

*Witty above her sex; but that's not all -*
*Wise to salvation was good Mistress Hall:*
*Something of Shakespeare was in that, but this*
*Wholly of Him with whom she is now in bliss.*

(inscription on the tombstone of Susanna Hall-Shakespeare; 1583-1649)

*Hall is laid here, very renowned*
*For his medical skill, looking for*
*The joys of the Kingdom of God.*
*Worthy was he, for his merits,*

(inscription on the tombstone of John Hall; 1575-1635)

(Hl. transl. from Latin, Fripp: Shakespeare, man & artist, II, p. 891, note 5)

## CONTENTS

| | Preface | 11 |
|---|---|---|
| I | The wedding date | 13 |
| II | Preparations | 17 |
| III | The marriage | 21 |
| IV | To bed with the bride | 25 |
| V | Summer 1607 | 29 |
| VI | Winter 1607 | 33 |
| VII | Christmas 1607 | 37 |
| VIII | Worries and faith | 41 |
| IX | Our Achilles heel | 45 |
| X | The four humors | 49 |
| XI | September 1608 | 55 |
| XII | Temptations | 59 |
| XIII | Melancholy at Saint Michael, 1610 | 63 |
| XIV | Summer of bad luck, 1613 | 67 |
| XV | The practice in our home | 73 |
| XVI | Fire and fight | 79 |
| XVII | A thoughtless marriage | 83 |
| XVIII | Master Shakespeare dies, April 1616 | 87 |
| XIX | A difficult Christmas | 93 |
| XX | Susanna and Laetitia, farewell to the Greenes | 99 |
| XXI | Puritan troubles | 103 |
| XXII | The Maypole and the Mayflower | 109 |
| XXIII | An old friendship and an ill wife | 115 |
| XXIV | Mother Anne is dead | 119 |
| XXV | Susanna is orphaned and Shakespeare's work collected | 125 |
| XXVI | Eliza ill | 131 |
| XXVII | Eliza marries | 137 |
| XXVIII | Hall churchwarden and Susanna ill again | 143 |
| XXIX | Great pressure on Hall | 147 |
| XXX | Doctor Hall himself ill | 151 |
| XXXI | Pews and ladies | 155 |

| | | |
|---|---|---|
| XXXII | More melancholy | 159 |
| XXXIII | Hall's worries and the plague once again | 163 |
| XXXIV | Hall deceased | 167 |

Postscript 171

Appendix A: The Shakespeare Family Tree 175

Appendix B: Stratford-upon-Avon in the time of Susanna Shakespeare 176/177

Acknowledgements 179

Quotes 181

Important sources 185

Literary references 187

# PREFACE

One can find an abundance of literature on the life and works of William Shakespeare. There is much less to read about the life of his eldest daughter Susanna and her husband, John Hall.

In this book **SUSANNA SHAKESPEARE** I have tried to describe her life from the viewpoint of a woman in Stratford in the first half of the seventeenth century. I have as carefully as possible associated with the life of Susanna the life of her illustrious father, that of her famous husband doctor Hall plus the medical knowledge of the time.

I have retained most of the data from the cases of the patients of Hall, which he wrote in Latin in his *Select Observations on English Bodies of Eminent Persons in desperate Diseases*. However I have dated a few before 1611 for the purpose of the story, as one assesses that the observations are just described from that date onwards.

The observations of the patients by John Hall can all be found in the books of Joan Lane and Harriet Joseph, under the relating names of the clients. The text of the letter by Sir Sidney Davenport in my Chapter XIX is also in those two books.

In the description of the cases from the notes of John Hall himself I have followed the translation by doctor Cooke, as printed at Harriet Joseph and Joan Lane. Where necessary, I have gratefully consulted the enlightening explanations by Joseph and Lane. Especially the descriptions of the medication and the background of the treated persons by Joan Lane were of great help. (See her Index of Drugs and Preparations / Index of Persons).

The Shakespeare quotes are from Stanley Wells' WILLIAM SHAKESPEARE, The complete works, 1988.

I cherished and will always cherish the very carefully composed books of the late Mr. E.I. Fripp, particularly his 'SHAKESPEARE, Man & Artist', part I and II of 1938, edited after his death in 1931, as also his 'Shakespeare's STRATFORD' of 1928.

When I started reading and translating, I could not have imagined that I was about to set out on a 'journey' of ten years. This began by going deeply into Shakespeare, England and Stratford in the sixteenth and seventeenth century. As meticulously as possible I have let myself be guided by the data in the most important books.

However, the inner life of the named persons, all of whom actually have existed, I had to fill in for the most part by means of those data plus my own imagination. The fact that I could in doing so draw upon my personal experiences as an assisting wife in the practice at home of my psychiatrist husband, has facilitated and deepened my empathy with Susanna Shakespeare and her John Hall.

# I
# THE WEDDING DATE

It will be on a Friday in the month of the early roses. To be precise on the fifth of June of the year sixteen hundred and seven. The big day, when John and I will say 'I do'!

"Do you John Hall, son of Mistress and Master William Hall from Bedfordshire, physician, gentleman, take as your lawful wife Susanna Shakespeare, daughter of Anne Hathaway and William Shakespeare, playwright, actor and gentleman in Stratford?"

John himself is a physician too. He had to exercise this profession for at least three years in his own hometown first. And now he has a practice in our town of Stratford and is also a consultant at stately houses in the area. When he first started work here, most people waited to see which way the cat jumped. You never know. Everyone can call himself a doctor. But soon he won respect, my John, of the ordinary people too - of all the people.

In fact he does not actually call himself a doctor. He needed some other qualifications. He is an MA, Master of Arts – not an MD, Doctor of Medicine that is. Master Hall sounds good enough, he finds, and people here call him doctor anyhow. He has studied, with his elder brother Dive, in Cambridge. There John matriculated at the age of fourteen, to Queens college. He has also travelled widely abroad, across the sea, on the continent. He has learned so much. How the human body works. What kind of diseases a person can get. Which medications work best. How to fabricate them out of herbs and other resources. Where you can find or order them. What you should never apply because it's downright dangerous, or even deadly. How fast you have to deal with it, or how long you have to wait and be patient. To which symptoms you should pay attention. It's too much to mention. And then you really learn most in practice, says John. It comes not only from the books, and there is no royal road to it.

His own father, William Hall, has been able to pay for those studies, with eleven children... He is not without means. He owns land in Bedfordshire, and also in Acton, Middlesex. But still it will not have been easy, especially not when his wife passed away, John's mother. Maybe they had the support of their family coat of arms, and lived up to that image, which is a bit grim. Three large heads of white hounds with drooping ears and a huge mouth with teeth. But I had to laugh at it too. Does that say something about your family, darling?

Our family is really small then when you compare, all things considered. Father, mother, my only sister Judith and I. Our brother Hamnet died, when he was just eleven years old. If only he could have been here these days. I should just not think about it now.

So my John comes from a large family. He was born in fifteen hundred seventy five in Carlton in Bedfordshire. He is close on eight years older than I am. With father and mother it is just the other way around. Funny actually. Father was so young when I came. He was only eighteen when he and Anne had to get married because I was already three months on the way. I must have been in a hurry. Weird idea: my dear is only just eleven years younger than father. Master Shakespeare appreciates him. It shows. Formerly he would sometimes poke fun at doctors. Nothing more jolly than that. But since he knows Hall he is a little bit more cautious and at least satisfied with our commitment.

That is perhaps reflected in father's most recent play Pericles. The doctor, Cerimon, will bring the wife of Prince Pericles of Tyre, Thaisa, who had been presumed dead, back to life. The doctor comes off well this time - he is a doctor who doesn't care a thing about wealth, who always has his purse open and strives only for good. That fragment is, to say the least, flattering to a doctor. Hall would not dare to say this of himself. He is not involved with that at all, my groom. Or was it just a bit of cynicism by father? That ever open purse - not opened to give but to receive?

Anyway, there is so much to prepare for the fifth. Wedding clothes, of course. And food and drinks. Wine and beer, as much as possible for the guests. And there should be music too. It will be a merry feast. For everyone, family, friends, neighbours and acquaintances.

The poorer people should be able to get a piece of the pie too. For some time now it has been so turbulent in our Stratford. Everywhere there are crowded meetings. People are angry and dissatisfied. Whole sites are being fenced off and farmworkers are driven away. The landlord, sir Edward Greville, operates in a rough and ready harsh manner. He belongs to the wealthy family of Warwick Castle, but he always is short of money with his way of living. He wants to have the meadows for himself, for sheep, because the wool brings in so much. So he is keeping the site surrounded by hedges and ditches, to keep out the ordinary farmer. That makes for bad blood.

There is no respite from this anymore since Queen Elizabeth died four years ago and King James succeeded her. I beg your pardon for saying this - we ought to have respect for the King - but he still must find his way. Of course it is not easy to succeed such a powerful Queen. People like this landlord therefore feel free to act ever more aggressively against the poor people. But those hard-working men and women are putting up with this no longer. They are sticking together. They pull down the fences and destroy the hedges. The governors have been instructed to stop them. And if they don't want to listen, they come down on them with a heavy hand. Then they can be captured. Even in our Guild Hall, one should take into consideration that there could be a place for prisoners. The treasure-chest could be taken away from the armory. And they want to restore the wooden block, so that one can be placed on view for everyone to see them with their head and hands in the wooden thing. Poor people. So much injustice. Who will fight for them? If only I could invite them all to our wedding. Such a day is not for you alone.

Meanwhile the patients always come first of course. Today Margaret Kempson came running in, daughter of miller Sadler from Churchstreet. She had a horrible pain from a hollow tooth. Hall grumbled though. First they try everything themselves. They swallow all kinds of drugs and use all sorts of charms, and if apparently nothing is found to help, they come to him with their tail between their legs.

Two fluid ounces of analgesic water of the corn poppy, he prescribed, and oil of vitriol, as much as was necessary to make it sharp. In it had to be dipped lint, gauze of linen or cotton. Margaret had to keep this every time in and against the hollow tooth. The pain subsided quickly, but the poor woman also had such a headache. For this Hall prescribed pills with aloe and a purgative gum resin. Then half a scruple of slices of larch agaric, that's some kind of mushroom, and betony water. Seven pills had to be made out of it. It worked well. Margaret had ten stools and three vomits. At the same time as the stools four big long worms came out free. And thus, Hall said, she was freed from her symptoms.

In the meantime the summer is hot and dry. The harvests are failing as we had to contend with major floods in January. Many think that this is the anger of God. That the people have not been God-fearing enough. Hall has his heart in his throat. Usually such weather conditions predict nothing good. An epidemic with vomiting and diarrhea could break out easily. We hope and pray that it is not forthcoming this time. That the marriage time will be granted to us and that it will be a feast. Then my doctor will be at everyone's disposal again.

# II
# PREPARATIONS

As far as clothing goes Hall likes to keep it sober. That is the way he is. He does not want to waste. Not even on his wedding day. He will be dressed in black, as befits a Puritan. That will be warm in this clammy summer - white is cooler to wear, and I must say that it is also on the pricey side, black clothing. The darker the clothes, the more expensive, because then they must repeatedly be dyed. This in contrast to natural shades of course. But this is expenditure he is sure he wants to make, then again it will help to make a distinguished impression. Perhaps that also suits him best, and will show his figure and shape favorably. I think he is a beautiful man. Imposing and proud. Someone who knows what he wants. Without further ado. So for him no finely crafted leather shoes. No scalloped edges and slits along the waist, the neck and the shoulders. No padded trunk hose with decorative piping and all the frills. The only luxury he will want to put up with are his gloves of fine scented leather, such as grandfather used to make. Grandfather Shakespeare was a tanner and white leather glove maker. He tanned the skin of horses and deer, dogs and sheep. He traded in wool too. For a long time, he had great prestige. He also has been alderman in our city and that reflected highly on the family.

But what about me though, Hall, I asked. Can I adorn myself on my wedding day, for this once?

Thus I'm going to be the most beautiful bride, you can imagine. I'll have starched cuffs and pleated linen and lace collars. Narrow slippers from the finest leather, with small indentations and embroidery. Colored petticoats and handmade silk knee-length stockings. A tight pair of bodices, stiffened with whalebones and pull cords, nice and straight. Soft quilted underclothes with the laces on the sides fastened tight. And over that the most radiant bridal gown, you've ever seen. Through the little bit of lead white on my cheeks I'll blush, hoping that my Hall will forgive me the extravagance, and will never forget the beauty of that day.

That night I dreamt that everyone was present. Father and mother, their friends Judith and Hamnet Sadler, who are the godparents of my brother and sister, who were named after them at baptism. Our own Judith I also saw and very vaguely our Hamnet, also present, but he had remained small. I think that's the great thing about dreams, that you sometimes see your deceased loved ones again for a little while. And still as bright, as if you really can touch them and talk with them. Then they have been with you, if only for a moment.

Thus I saw the two Judiths and Hamnets, and the family of John of course. His father and his brother and sisters. His older brother Dive I saw very clearly. And also their friend, Matthew Morris, assistant and confidant of John's father, who came to Stratford with my John.

And there I also saw standing together Abraham Sturley, Thomas Greene and Richard Quiney, all on very friendly terms with father and with each other. What an honor that they were there, the learned gentlemen, who are and were of so much importance to our city. Sturley is a lawyer and solicitor for our town. He has also been bailiff here, but that was before John came to Stratford. It is true that he is much older than my dear, but he has studied in Cambridge too, so there are strong ties between them. We like him so much. We just think that he has done his best for John so that he could settle here as a doctor. Our dear Thomas Greene addresses father as 'coz', cousin. He also is a lawyer and city clerk of Stratford. And Richard Quiney, linen draper by profession, was bailiff here twice. He had great respect, because he represented our town several times at the court of our former Queen.

All friends, neighbors and acquaintances were present, but it was just these three that really stood out strongly. Once Sturley, Quiney and Greene went, all three of them, when it was necessary, to the Bishop of Worcester. They sought the help of the Bishop against that miserable Sir Edward Greville, who keeps trying to chip away at the rights of our city. The Bishop then came to Stratford, and has calmed people's emotions.

And one time Quiney and Sturley negotiated in London to reduce the toll charges, when our city could not cope with them after the big fires in fifteen ninety-four and ninety-five. Stratford suffered terribly. There was great distress, because of those fires, the terrible plague had created havoc and times were hard in agriculture. The three gentlemen could arrange many things for our borough, so people didn't have to pay so much.

But there were also more cheerful meetings. Then father brought stories about their meals together. A man must eat, and how can that be done better than in good company.

Next morning I woke up with moist eyes. I realized immediately that it had been a dream. Quiney has already been dead for five years. When he stood up once again for the population against Greville, he had been beaten up at night by a drunken group of supporters of the wretch, and succumbed to his injuries. And of course our dear Hamnet died eleven years ago. I tried to lie as still as possible and to concentrate, to keep hold of them, until they slipped away, and I had to get up.

John had already left early in the morning for patients in the surrounding areas. He visits them especially in Worcester, Gloucester, Northampton and Ludlow. Those areas are between twenty-six and sixty miles riding from us. Thus he travels far on horseback to his consultations at the larger country houses and castles.

When servants are ill there he treats them too. My husband does not make any distinctions. He is committed to young and old, rich and poor, man and woman, Protestant and Catholic.

Thus he also took care of John Winter, eldest son of the Catholic Robert Winter, who was, at the end of sixteen hundred and five, closely involved in the so-called Gunpowder Plot. Father Winter was one of the peers who had intended to blow up Parliament in London, during the opening by King James. They had been so furious with the measures of the government, which had to mitigate Catholic influences as much as possible. The leaders of the uprising came to meet a horrible end.

Now this son John Winter was cruelly tormented with worms and fever. Hall told me how he has treated him. First the patient was given a suppository, made of honey. Then he had to drink the decoction of prepared and raw hartshorn and there was applied to his navel a poultice against worms, with rue, wormwood and aloe. He was purged with half a fluid ounce of manna, which is the sweet juice of trees from warm southern areas, which was dissolved in broth. It resulted in many dead worms in stinking excrement. He took in his food and drink powder of precious coral, pearl, hartshorn and garnet, plus pieces of the gems sapphire, emerald and ruby, mixed with a little piece of gold leaf. He had to take against coughing a syrup of the plants poppy and maidenhair. With these medicines, he was, with God's blessing, cured in three days.

My John gets to see inside the most beautiful houses. The house that John Winter had inherited from his father is the most charming house in Worcestershire. In that area live very many Catholics but also many leading Puritan families. The fashionable mansion is in a romantic place, so isolated that you can feel safe there if you're on the run. The building has ten rooms on the ground floor and even more upstairs, and it provides two hiding places for priests. The family was wealthy enough to pay the fines for being recusant, when they had not attended divine service once again.

That is still a bit different with us. Last year I was also fined because of absence in church. Immediately the story went around, as gossip does in a village. It was said I would be popishly affected or a church-papist, who only occasionally goes to church in order to avoid a fine.

Oh well, I let them say what they want. We are not poor, certainly not, and also we live very well. But as rich as the Winters we are not and I will obediently show my face henceforth on Sunday. That's not so bad anyway.

# III
# THE MARRIAGE

What I was afraid of happened. No epidemic, but shortly before the wedding day Hall was sent for by Mr Brown, a Roman priest. May be the name of the good man was different, because in order to protect themselves and also their followers Catholic recusants often take on other names. The man suffered from typhoid fever and was in agony. My husband to be gave him six drachm, six little pinches, of the hefty emetic against tertian fever, two drachm syrup of violets and one fluid ounce of bittersweet of squill. Once mixed this had to be administered and it then caused the patient to vomit five times and to pass four stools.

The next day, the treatment continued with bloodletting, purging and an enema. To quench his thirst the patient got a cool drink, but that was soon gone. Hall had to find another solution so he then tried the previously applied powder of all kinds of gems, called 'species liberant', spring water and burnt hartshorn. This he had to scum and clarify with the whites of eggs. Of course that detained him a great deal, but it worked.

Confident that he had been to all lengths and in the hope that the man would soon be put right, my John came home to change his clothes and join me and our guests.

We went in procession to our church, Trinity Church, through the beloved streets of our Stratford, with the families, friends, neighbors and those interested. I felt beautiful in my skirt of fine worsted and gown of home-woven sheep wool. I had been afraid that it would be too hot on that day, but the natural materials were also cooling. My long hair had been combed and endlessly brushed and hung shiny on to my shoulders. The musicians, who led the way, played exciting tunes. Groomsmen accompanied us with lace ribbons and rosemary.

Behind us walked the unmarried girls from the village, with wedding cakes and wreaths of fine gilded wheat. It's like you look at your dear streets and houses on such a day with very different and new eyes: the family home, our lovely 'New Place', Chapel Street, the Guild Hall, our school and the almshouses in Old Town, the old part of our town. There we imagine our dream house with horse stables and all. A house with gabled roofs and walls of oak wood with plaster. With a spacious entrance hall and a wide oak staircase. A large kitchen overlooking a lush walled garden. There will be flowers and herbs, culinary herbs and medicinal ones in abundance. And, of course, a place for the study and consulting-room of John, with a small dispensary at home. Wouldn't that be wonderful? Music for the future.

Then we went through the Churchway, between the two rows of trees to the northern gate of our church of the Holy Trinity. A trusted area of calm and contemplation, where I was baptized on Sunday the twenty-sixth of May fifteen eighty three, on Trinity Sunday. And now I will marry – as if your life may begin again, or so it feels. Will everything be any different from now on? I had a wonderful childhood. Mother has taken care of us so well - nothing was too much for her. But Hamnet's death cast a heavy shadow on our lives. She has never quite been the same anymore. And from that day forward I have lost my innocence as a child forever. Judith then also changed greatly. Her better half she had to let go at such a young age and that leaves its scars. Father, when he came home, could not muster up the looseness and gaiety, which he otherwise always brought in the house. His son and heir had been lost.

Hamnet has been baptized here also, along with Judith, on the second of February, two years after me. Of course, Judith and Hamnet Sadler were present that day too. In turn, they had their son, who was born thirteen years later, named after father, William. Father has in the year of the death of our Hamnet written the play King John. There are a couple of poignant lines in it about a deceased son. Mother Constance says, if I remember correctly, in the third act, fourth scene:

*'Grief fills the room up of my absent child,
Lies in his bed, walks up and down with me,
Puts on his pretty looks, repeats his words,
Remembers me of all his gracious parts,
Stuffs out his vacant garments with his form;'*

And a little further:

*'O Lord, my boy, my Arthur, my fair son,
My life, my joy, my food, my all the world,
My widow-comfort, and my sorrow's cure!'*

No one else can write it down the way father can. The moisture of tears comes behind your eyes just like that ... But where was I - my wedding day. We had arrived at the church. We stopped in front of the inner door with the large metal knocker, which I could draw by heart. It represents a man's head with a little cap on. He has a sad, grim expression, but also he expresses serenity and quiet resignation. How many people will have touched him in the course of time, in their joy or sadness? At funerals, regular divine services, baptisms or weddings, such as ours.

"For better - for worse, in sickness - in health, for richer - for poorer". The most beautiful lovers' vow that exists in the whole world. If you fare well or badly, during illness or health, in wealth or if you are poorer – you should continue to love each other just as much. This will make or break the whole togetherness of two people. "I, John Hall, take thee, Susanna Shakespeare, to be my wedded wife".

We kissed each other before the very eyes of all those present in the crowded church. And they clapped and laughed. All tension disappeared from me when wine was served, as a sign of good friendship between the two families. And although some may rather want to skip this habit, all our guests raised their glass to our happiness.

Then we went in the same parade back to New Place for further celebrations. I felt privileged that father had been able to make rousing and sweet little plays and songs. Everyone who wanted to could participate. We couldn't hold back our tears, John and I, and I also saw our parents rubbing their eyes. I looked forward to handing out the many gifts, which we had made or purchased for the guests.

Every now and then John threw his arms around me and we looked each other in the eyes, for the first time as a brand new doctor- and doctor's wife couple.

Meanwhile John received the message that the Roman priest had revived well. Later my Hall would write in his notes that the Catholic man recovered beyond expectations, especially with the decoction of hartshorn, with which he had cured this and other fevers in a short time. I admired him that he could bring about all this. We embraced, as though holding each other for the first time. Our hearts were almost pounding against each other. The exciting adventure could begin.

# IV
# TO BED WITH THE BRIDE

How busy and noisy they all were. They had of course a good drop too much, our friends. They brought us to the bedroom, which had been carefully put in order. Crisp spotless linen, embroidered so imaginatively, graced our bed.

The drinks helped the ambiguous jokes get going. Calling and singing and screaming, they are pretty good at it! Especially, when John's witnesses had to pull down my garters, by tradition. Just in time I had those loosened myself first and I had them already dangling down, against any hands which may have grabbed too much. A weird custom actually. A strange shudder ran down my back, along with a feeling of excitement, mixed with shame. Funny to see the gentlemen tie my stockings to their hats. My bridesmaids were beyond themselves with giggling, while they carried me towards the bed in the meantime. We still had the giggles when they helped me undress.

Off went the beautiful wedding gown. Would I never wear it again? We had worked on it for so many days. With throbbing heart and with so much expectation it had been well cared for down to the last detail. Tried on time and again, until it fitted perfectly to the girl's body, which was going to be that of a woman now. The shiny ribbons were one by one unbuttoned. The rushing outerwear carefully taken off, despite the elated mood, and then onto the wafer-thin underwear. My mother, my aunt, sister and girlfriends sighed, that they never had seen such an enchanting bride. I myself could feel a touch of melancholy and took a deep breath.

In the next room John's companions helped him undress. That could have gone faster than with me, but the men almost suffocated in their own silliness. One was apparently even filthier with his comments than the other. The men didn't want to play second fiddle in the parade of folly. Imagination bolts to the honeymoon suite mercilessly, under the influence of wine, beer, fatigue and fun.

Thereupon they released my 'husband' - how does that sound - in his nightshirt to me. What a fuss! The room was now chock-full. My girlfriends came up out of the room and then suddenly ran back again. John's witnesses grabbed my stockings, and my bridesmaids grabbed John's. Both parties went to sit on the foot of our bed and swung the stockings around above their heated heads and threw them towards us. They landed just on top of our heads, and that's a good sign for the pitchers. They will quickly end up married, so it is said, and perhaps to each other!

In the meantime they cooked caudle with milk, sugar, cinnamon, nutmeg and egg yolks. With a solemn gesture it was handed over to us then. I don't know whether that's better for fertility? We did swallow the slippery stuff but fast. Brrrr!

And now John in his turn had to call those troublesome gents all sorts of names. And I, as a bride, kept my mouth shut demurely. Finally, according to time-honored custom, the fresh husband jumps up in his shirt and drives everyone out of the door. And so this my hero did too.

Here we were then. Alone at last. When I dared to look, I saw John still standing in his undershirt and underpants. I myself held the beautiful sheets up to my chin. Never had I felt so exposed. I, who was so proud of my breasts, who wanted to show them so much to him and to have them felt, who had experienced this moment a hundred times in my head, I cast down my eyes, and waited with pounding heart.

Prudently Hall opened the bedclothes on his side of the bed. He went gently beside me and grabbed my fingers. Hand in hand we lay and listened to the ebbing festivities. Rest. For a while an enormous fatigue overtook me and at the same time my eyes became moist. How great it all had been. A celebration never to forget. What days. What a day. Now we are forever noted as a couple in the register of the Church: '' Junij 5 John Hall gentleman & Susanna Shaxpere ''. How wonderful is that?

Mr. P. flashes upon me now, with his 'flux semen', that is spontaneous ejaculation. There are people who persistently have it, Hall once told me. My husband can deal with that too. If he describes such a delicate case then in the evening in his books, he notes the name of the patient incompletely and he gives only the initials. For this man's problems Hall prescribed a purgative, with the pulp of the fruits of cassia, which is a Chinese cinnamon, and tamarind, the fruit of a tropical tree, also known as 'asem'. It has a sweet and sour taste and it smells rather nice. This purged the gentleman well. Then a pill had to be made with syrup of the gum of the Asian plant tragacanthus, which has a soothing effect. This along with Armenian amber, mummy powder and the jaw of a pike, of each two scruples. Mummy powder, powder of a mummy — of this one says that it can penetrate into all parts of the body, that it restores the worn limbs, heals consumptions and ulcers, counteracts blood coagulation and stops flow of blood and rheums. And the jaw of the pike is recommended to reduce fevers and to combat the plague. He also had to drink steeled milk, which is milk prepared with rust, which is constipating. The Greek physician Dioscorides had already prescribed this around the year sixty after Christ. He was the greatest in the field of medicinal plants in antiquity. He has described all this in his ' De materia medica'. I always try to remember it well when my Hall tells me about this background information.

So it is like that to lie down as husband and wife. So familiar and strange and hot and cold. We turn our bodies towards each other. How beautiful you are – all I have dreamed of, whispers John. He kisses my tear-stained face. And I return it. Our limbs nestle against each other. Skin to skin, that's…., that seems, as if there is no place and no time anymore. Fatigue can find a way out. And it feels better than the uncontrollable lust of a few weeks earlier, which surprised me so… Let's leave it at that…

The following day, the sixth of June, I wore my hair pinned up, as a married woman does, covered with a colorful embroidered bonnet. People address me now as 'mistress'. Such special experiences, you might want to write it all down. '' For better - for worse, in sickness - in health. To love and to cherish - till death do us part…"

# V
# SUMMER 1607

In London the plague reigns. It's getting worse and worse. If you're not careful, you get infected as a matter of course. People simply die in the streets, they say, so how do you run away from that. I worry most about father. He'll better be off but still soon there. The theatres have to close now, thank goodness. Of course there are always too many people gathered there. I heard that father's company will go on tour.

They will also call at Oxford and Cambridge. Father has many friends in Oxford. He comes there regularly, because it is situated just between London and Stratford.

Father is staying frequently at the Davenants, in their lodging house at the Corn Market. Master Davenant is fond of him and of his plays. He is a Puritan, and at the same time he is a great admirer of Shakespeare's work. You see, that that can go together very well, Hall. You can be an ardent Puritan and yet acknowledge the value and beauty of stage-work. And you can just admit it too. A little flexibility does no harm. Master Davenant is discreet and serious, loves his books very much, and moreover it is also a lively household there. Mistress Davenant is very cheerful and a handsome sparkling woman. Father is particularly fond of her. The couple has quite a number of small children, and Mistress Davenport is, I believe, pregnant again. It's a nice family. Little Robert is five years young and told that master Shakespeare had given him a hundred kisses. Their second son is just one year old. Shakespeare is his godfather, and the sprout has been baptized William. Will father have told them, that his own eldest daughter is also expecting?

They have such a beautiful room on the second floor, says father, which overlooks the bustling Corn Market. Above the colorful wallpaper runs a frieze round the walls, with ornate black letters, with which God is praised in verse. I don't know who wrote that, but

I'll bet, that father could have written that even more thoughtfully. He sure can write. I wish I could. Sometimes I feel an urge to express myself on paper. I can philosophize endlessly about how such a thing works, because I also try it myself on the quiet.

Writing and rhyming – it has to come out of the caverns of your soul. Out of the obscure and the brightest sides of your brain. Out of moments of inattention. Out of a twilight state. Out of just not being awake. That is when the imagination gets to work. Unremarkably she is at her best, or is it a he? Like when you're highly flushed with fever and in bed and actually don't want to think about anything. More or less like that. Then the phrases and thoughts come to existence, that appeal to that layer - or else at a spectator or reader - which is just below the consciousness. The word says it: the subconscious. And then there's the recognition. That is what appeals. On a blank sheet of paper it is the hardest. It is better if there are already a few sentences on it, or a drawing.

I'm on my bed for a while. If I lay my hands on my fourth month belly, nothing can disturb the peace and quiet. Nothing I have to do anymore. If I breathe deeply, I can relax. Happiness. I hear the sounds in the house. So comforting. A world, which for a moment should be able to run without me. I saw to it that everything is done that needed to be done. The entrance is clean. That is important. The steps and the floors are swept. The dispensary, with all its mortars and glazed pots, is decent. The notes made by John are put in order. I can come to rest for a while safely. They have to manage without me this afternoon.

It's wonderful, to listen to the sounds in our home. The hubble-bubble of the servants. The hustle and bustle of the practice. The comings and goings of people, day after day, with their requests for help. Footsteps. Doors that slam. Steps that crack. Voices. Voices with their intonation. How much can you gather from that … everything actually. Perhaps more than out of words. Quarrelling and anger, hesitation and reassurance. Interim silences. Regular talk and small talk. Chitchat and hot air. Conviviality and severity. Gravity and announcement of disease, of serious disorder and of death.

You can also fall ill when you are pregnant. Hall also helps pregnant women who are suffering from diarrhea and are vomiting. Then he takes special care with treatment. You should not promote stools and vomiting again. And he is very reluctant anyway with bloodletting. Then he gives 'sack', a light sweet wine, and this mixed with a little oil of vitriol. Of that the woman must take a liquid ounce in the morning for a week and eat not too much food. Hall anoints the belly with oil of wormwood then, and 'mace', a spice made from the dried peel of the nutmeg. This is mixed with half a drachm of 'species aromaticum rosatum', a mixture of red roses and spices. That warms and strengthens the stomach. Such an ointment is harmless and beneficial.

He has anointed the pregnant mistress Boughton with that recently. She had complaints of vomiting and diarrhea too. She had six ounces of the 'sack' prescribed with six drops of the oil of vitriol. She took an ounce of it each morning on an empty stomach. She was healed, God be praised.

I sure would like to have my belly rubbed in with that ointment too. But Hall believes: as long as all goes well, we undertake nothing. Let nature do its work. I don't think that I can bear such intimacy of him with another pregnant woman. You are extra sensitive, Hall said, which is all part of it too. But when he saw how sad I was then, he has anointed my belly with all tenderness that was in him, with the same liniment.

You can also die in childbirth, together with the infant. Unfortunately that's still common. When the baby lies back to front for instance and is just before birth not lying properly with the head down, then it becomes difficult. But I don't want to think about that. Not with the new life under my heart.

The heavier voice of my husband I hear now. The balance and prevalence resounds. The obvious tone, with which he goes to meet the people. He has that from natural bent. They can count on him. He has the gift of calming people, with his knowledge. And in doing so, he accepts the other person as he or she is. When they leave our house, they usually feel a bit better already.

Thus I can hear, if the consultation will still last for a while, or that he's rounding off. Then the intonation becomes raised a little bit. One is speaking louder suddenly. I have learned to recognize this. I know it perfectly. Sure enough, now I hear the door open again.

Geniality. Safety. Deeply snuggled away under the covers. I feel my temples beating from fatigue. Just as long as all continues to go well with the new life. But with this husband next to me, nothing can go wrong. Did the belly move a bit now? And now more violently. As if it says: take it easy, mum, it is all right in here. Funny feeling, such a light bumping belly. It feels soft and comfortable and familiar. But also so new and exciting. And it does not hurt at all. It is rather as if you are cradled yourself. I'm sure I will never forget this lovely feeling.

# VI
# WINTER 1607

Hall's father has died. Exactly six months after our wedding. John is now an orphan. That he could do nothing more for him, troubles him so. We as humans are powerless in the face of death, if it is God's will, he says. Though you can still be a hundred times a doctor and know about a thousand medicines and herbs. Your time is your time. Death is death. He felt so cold, his father. Colder than stone. How can that be so all of a sudden, after you have felt warm your whole life.

It is so wintery outside. Long icicles hang off the roofs, and snow covers the entire country. My dear is sad. Even though he and his father did not always agree, it is nevertheless still hard when you know you will have to miss each other forever. Fighting also was their way of bonding and it seems John is working harder and harder, to cope with it. I myself can do little. My big belly is in the way. Father-in-law will not be able to experience the new life. On the twelfth of December he has still made his will in Acton and then it only took a while.

He is bequeathing all his books on medicine to John. But his books on astronomy and astrology he leaves to his confidant, our Matthew Morris. Provided that Matthew will familiarize John with the books, bearing in mind this benevolent gift of his master. But this is only if John will seriously lose himself in the said learning and want to study it deeply. Furthermore Morris also gets all his books on alchemy. William Hall knew very well, that John wants to keep himself far away from that and that he thinks it is outdated and too unscientific.

Father Hall also left Matthew four pounds and that's a goodly amount. In addition is to his eldest son, our brother-in-law Dive, just forty shillings bequeathed. Father-in-law thought that Dive had provided him with too much trouble, and that he had long ago used up his part. The old man had not forgotten that he had had no support whatsoever from him after the early death of mother-in-law. Furthermore he also leaves forty shillings to the poor people of Acton.

Also Hall's sisters Elizabeth, Damaris, Sara and Martha each receive a certain amount. Sara is also married to a doctor. He did not study together with John, but in Oxford. Two sisters of father Hall each receive twenty nobles, one of whom has to give that to her son. My sister-in-law Elizabeth should, moreover, also spend it on the education of her son William, as an apprentice, since they have let him stay at home too long, according to the old Hall. Plus twelve pounds to divide between her other three children.

Furthermore the maid Anne gets thirty shillings, to be paid to her within a month after his death.

All other goods, assets, houses and plots of land he leaves to John, whom he designates as his executor. If John would refuse the latter, then his brother Dive would have to perform this task and give to John fifty pound, with all medicine books. But father-in-law assumed that John would be the executor. He had the most confidence in him.

My John thinks it is an honor, but shrinks from the hard work and the difficulties, that such a command entails. It is in addition to the responsibilities of his work and that will be soon too much for him. I understand. He is so meticulous and finds that he must be there for his patients one hundred percent. He rather would have refused his father, but eventually he could not find it in his heart to do so, and on the twentieth of December he attended the legal verification of the will in London. Also the home in Acton, where John has been a physician the first three years, is assigned to us, but we handed that house over to Dive, who must after all reside somewhere too. He is and remains our brother and brother-in-law and we will help out, when needed.

So John will give all the alchemy books to Matthew Morris. The executor must also meet any debts to creditors, and of course pay the funeral expenses.

He still had everything well under control, father-in-law, who began to mention in his will that he was sick in body, but, God be thanked, still perfectly fine in terms of memory and understanding. The introduction of the will has an ultra-Protestant, Puritan character, just like the author of it and his son, my husband. However much they both could clash as regards medical opinions, they were reasonably in agreement about faith. The will begins like this:

*'In dei nomine Amen I, WILLIAM HALL of Acton*
*in the countye of Midd gentleman sicke in bodye*
*but of a perfect memorye and understanding*
*I thancke God, Do ordayne constitute and make*
*this my last will and testament in manner*
*and forme folowing'*

Beautiful old fashioned spelling yet. First, he wanted that his body was buried in the church of Acton if he died there or in a church elsewhere. Further he says he bequeaths his soul to the almighty God who created him, and who gave his Son to redeem him.

Father-in-law was, forgive me that I say this, pretty wilful and strict. Moreover he made no effort to hide that. I am convinced that he always refused to treat someone of another faith.

My John is different. As a doctor he works for all and every human being in this region. He is fully committed to wanting to cure both rich and poor. Lately there was a pauper, one Hudson, who suffered from a swimming in his head, called 'vertigo'. My Hall had ten liquid ounces of blood taken from the anterior vein of his right arm and gave him a strong purgative pill. This provided the good man with nine stools. Then he had a drachm of dried feces of peacocks for a night infused in white wine, after which the stuff was filtered. The man was supposed to take this for fourteen days, from new moon to full moon, and he was healed.

In addition, Hall attends, for example, the immensely rich Sir Packington, who was in favor with our previous head of state, Queen Elizabeth. Her Majesty made the man a Knight of Bath and gave him the monopoly on the manufacture of starch, making him really overwhelmingly wealthy. Hall treated the noble gentleman with the bitter senna, which restores the appetite. He let it mix with, among other things, ginger, mace and cinnamon to flavor it and reduce the gnawing feeling. With this he made a powder from which a drachm was dosed in broth. This healed the nobleman well, for which he thanked Hall and asked for the recipe.

In good conscience my husband will heal the sick, whoever they are, upon the healing of which of course the honor in the first place should be unto the Lord, such as Hall every time indicates:

'The praise be unto the Lord God'.

Hall also has as his motto: 'he, who practises medicine without course and method, sails without rudder and oars'. This could well be a sneer to his late old gentleman, who leaned on that study of alchemy and astrology. In any case, it is his reproach to the many quacks in our country, who palm off on the unsuspecting citizen the most terrible salves and drinks. And those people come off well too. Mankind likes to be deceived.

# VII
# CHRISTMAS 1607

It is already Christmas. We have decorated the house with branches and wreaths of holly and ivy. There are so many red berries this year between the green. They light up brightly because of the flickering little flames in the winter darkness. The whole house smells like resin and herbs, apples and pinecones. Up to Epiphany these are usually the finest days of the year. In our church and at home by the fireside the birth of the Holy Child is celebrated with prayer and song. It is the time to put more alms in the open hands of the beggars, to give each other presents and to chase away with dancing, cards and laughing the melancholy of the darkest months. All people assemble and seek warmth in the company of one another. The food will be good and excessive. There will be venison, rabbit, fish and poultry. Wine and beer will flow and loosen the tongues. You hear people saying 'Good cheer' and 'God be with you' all day in the market and in the streets.

All kind of things will get a chance to be the subject of conversation. The trade in malt by mother, with which I often help, and other matters. The condition of the roads, the yield of the tithes, the harvest of the past year, lawsuits and squabbles, gossip and backbiting and last but not least the circumstances concerning father's plays. I hope father will manage to come this year. That would be nice for mother and also for the others. Greene, his cousin, Laetitia and their children, sister Judith, John and I cannot wait to see him. Then the house will be full of life, then conversations will blaze away, there will be quips, jokes and laughs. Every year it is a pleasure to listen to that and to take part in it. All of us around the fireplaces, with a rosy complexion on our cheeks and just a feeling of happiness in our body.

But this year it feels doubly. Father-in-law has only recently died, while the little creature under my heart stirs itself evermore strongly.

They say that this always occurs: new life comes, old life goes. It makes you so wistful. Let me make sure that we take down again the ivy and the holly in time. On the fifth of January, on the eve of Epiphany, you should already have all the green out of your house, otherwise it will bring misfortune. They say you should free the tree spirits, which are in it, again. Only in this way there will be fresh new growth in spring. Now that I'm vulnerable I believe everything - you never know.

We do our best to tend the fires in the house, and burn a lot of candles. Snow is falling ceaselessly and is almost a snow storm. The air colors deep dark grey by day, almost black. It really is dreadful outside. They tell how in London the Thames is frozen completely. I sure would like to see that. Market stalls are just on the ice, right from one side to the other. Boats can of course not be sailing anymore and are drawn by boatswains or horses, as well as the carriages. And there is bowling and dancing on the slippery floor. Also bear-baiting, with dogs fighting against a bear, is there, with the animals slithering and slipping unaccustomed to it. That would also be dangerous for me and for our unborn child. The craziest stories spread like wildfire. It is said that a woman had intercourse on the ice, so that she could say, that she had received a child on 'old Father Thames'. Imagine, I wouldn't even dare to tell anyone something like that. A few men and women twirl nicely on skates of bone or wood, and buy themselves hot chestnuts at the stalls. It will be a beautiful picture.

Would father also have seen this beauty? He will be too busy, I guess. His company, the 'King's Men', plays again for a few days at court. And I think they must perform on the last day of December in the Globe again.

It must have been difficult for father. They have indeed played in the Globe in the afternoon. But in the morning they had to bury uncle Edmund, father's younger brother, in Southwark, London. South of the frozen Thames, where it was such a cheerful hustle and bustle. Weird to think that you can no longer take your loved one with you into the upcoming year. He was only twenty-seven, Edmund. He was also an actor. He lived in London close by father, near Silverstreet in Cripplegate. Poor uncle. That summer he had to bury his son Edward there. People say it was an 'Illegitimate child' but what does it matter. People judge just like that. But loss is loss. Grief is grief. Father and his friends have paid twenty shilling in the St. Saviour for uncle for the ringing of the great bell. They have sent him off properly.

Now father still has his brother Gilbert, who is forty-one, and a retailer in Stratford, and who is also frequently in London. And his brother Richard, who is thirty-two. And of course dear aunt Joan, who is married to hatter Hart. It's an amazing world, with life beside death. Hall's father and Edmund died in the coldest winter, you can imagine, and in me the new life is kicking to see the light. Fortunately, I still have mum and dad. I don't even want to think about it what it would be like if they also would not be able to welcome our baby.

I'm glad father will take things a bit easier. Over the last seven years he wrote as many as fourteen plays. Two every year. But now he wants to write either less, or together with others. It seems to be insanely demanding, writing plays. Especially under pressure of time, which is always the case. And it must succeed, and appeal to the public time after time. And to the court. That is another thing. You have to be very diplomatic. You can never offend someone there. You have to know exactly what they do and do not want to hear. And yet a play should never be boring. Father is good at it. All these years he managed to come up with something new again and again. But you can notice that he's getting older. You can also see it. He must succeed in the field of creation, as well as of business. He must earn his daily bread, for the entire company and their families, and also for us of course.

It may now be peace of mind for him, that his eldest daughter has got a roof over her head, as it is called. Safely married, and well off. A doctor in the family. And a serious doctor too. Father can tease him, about being usually so grave and conscientious, my John. Then he makes him a figure of fun, such as urban Londoners do with people from the provinces. He is making a mockery then of the remedies which his son-in-law prepares.

So last there was John Smith of Newham. The elder man was severely tormented with the retention of urine for three days. So the poor soul could just not pee. It was caused by 'the stone', that is to say by stones in the urethra, which blocked the whole procedure. The fact that he could not urinate at all endangered the life of the man. Hall told that already many things were tried by others, without any progress, and that they finally in desperation had called him.

Hall gave him the following recipe: six handfuls of winter cherry berries and three drachm of parsley seeds. These had to be cooked in a sufficient quantity of milk. With this a posset drink had to be made, of which the man had to take six liquid ounces. It has to be mixed with syrup of marshmallow according to the recipe of Fernelius, one ounce, and Holland powder, two drachm. The good man drank white wine in which one had infused mashed winter cherries.

And now it comes. To the region of the bladder, between the penis and the anus, was applied the following: a nice big onion and a clove of garlic, fried with butter and vinegar. You can imagine how one, after drinking, dealt with this information. That is just the thing for father, who knows the language of theatres and pubs. My Hall sure knows how to join in with this for a while, but then finished his own story. It was indeed applied like this and within an hour the patient produced his urine, along with stone and grit. And so the poor man got rid of that long, disastrous and eminent danger, for which they thanked God.

Father surely appreciates that. He is very fond of his son-in-law and proud that he has such a worthy profession. He knows that John is held in high regard in Stratford and the surrounding area. That is a great relief for a father and also for mother. That's what you hope for, with a view to a good future for your precious child. If the mutual relations are good, such as those we have, you can dream of love and happiness for your children. As well as of the heartbeat of a long-awaited grandchild!

# VIII
## WORRIES AND FAITH

A knock at the door, then you just wait for a while, and you hear the voices of the servants and errand boys, who bring the vials with urine. Then Hall checks the water carefully for color and structure and asks for the story behind it, for the disease symptoms. After that he usually makes a reliable diagnosis and decides which herbs and other remedies will best deal with the illness.

It has almost become second nature to me, to listen to the different voices of the clients. Stories, small fragments of lives or long-winded sentences, sometimes far too detailed, endless or confused. I cannot make head or tail of it. Sometimes cries of pain during the bloodletting, which he really doesn't carry out often, but usually when he does it his words are full of confidence.

Only occasionally is there anger and mistrust – a doctor should not think he knows everything – full of indomitable disillusion or agony. Then often follows a long silence. In face of death neither doctor or patient have any defense. Hall also gets upset sometimes in these cases. Then he comes in the kitchen, or where I am at that time. He talks to me to get it out of his head. I take his side, but also think about it profoundly. I try to stay critical and he knows and appreciates that. Thus deliberation remains valuable. So I can flatter myself with the thought that I can be of help to him.

I call myself to order, when I prick up my ears upon hearing female voices, and listen out to the mutual tone. Because you never know - not so much with my John maybe, but it still may be possible with some ladies, who find the doctor at least an interesting figure. He is not at it himself, my John. He is fully focused on his profession. He tries to help everyone by paying them all his attention.

In addition, he wants to be as faithful as possible. He is interested in stories which father brings from London about strict Protestant people.

But this is better remaining secret. Those Puritans have advanced plans to go to Holland, to the capital of Amsterdam. They think that the situation overseas is better for being sound in faith. They feel that each congregation of believers should be independent, and not fall under the authority of the state church, as is the case here. One John Robinson from Norwich has taken the lead in this group. He feels that the so-called Reformation did not go far enough and that too many Catholic habits and rituals have remained. Habits that our grandparents still cherished and that are rooted in our society. In the Guildhall grandfather Shakespeare even had to paint a thin layer of whitewash on the wall paintings of the Day of Judgment, hoping maybe that it could be washed off later on. Real Puritans would not have wanted that image to be shown ever again. Thus they neither want the sign of the cross to be made above infants at baptism, or that the midwife can baptize a baby herself, when it is in mortal danger. They want to dismiss incompetent clerics, which seems logical to me. And priests should be allowed to marry, as they were allowed to under Edward VI, which I find reasonable. An end must be put to the personal enrichment of ecclesiastical magistrates and not before time! But what I do find difficult is that you may not gain too much knowledge - that would feed the sin of pride. And pride - that I know - you should avoid. I don't find that easy. I am so proud of my John and the child who is coming.

My body is getting thicker and my breasts fuller. My size changes every day. Hall says he likes me like this. He has always found pregnant women beautiful. Beautiful and moving. How can I not be proud? Modest gratitude is possible too, says John then. I will practice. A lot goes through my mind since I have been pregnant. All sorts of weird thoughts too and they jump from one subject to another.

Did it never occur to you, John, in relation to other women? You see so many. You talk to them, look at them. You are watching them, like no other is allowed to watch them. You touch them in places I would rather not think about. Then my breathing becomes oppressed. You give them so much attention. And you see them and you are familiar with them.

I dare not speak out to him. It sounds so selfish. Not so noble and nice. Do I think like this because of my blessed circumstance?

I do know what he would answer: 'Susanna, it's my job. So you should not think like that. It's totally not what you are making of it. I approach it professionally, and that is the way I look at my clients. What do you get into your head? We doctors are seriously trained. Do you really think that there is room and opportunity for such ulterior thoughts. And it is also strictly prohibited according to the oath that we have made, the oath of Hippocrates, who was the most famous ancient Greek physician. On that oath you have to swear that all you have learned in the medical field, you will apply to the best of your ability. That you will prescribe no deadly medicine to anyone, nor will give any such advice. There is also the rule, that upon entering a dwelling one is required to refrain from any deliberate wrongdoing, in particular from sexual intercourse with women and men, either free persons or slaves. That was written already in former times, around the year 400 before Christ. And of course then followed the requirement of professional secrecy.'

Sure, I know all that. As his wife and confidante I also keep in mind that I don't let my tongue run away with someone, which is not always easy. Forgive me, Hall. It just comes upon me lately. Everything is in the way. My own thoughts too, and I'm afraid. Afraid I will get ill and will catch a fever just before or after giving birth.

Puerperal fever. It is often only clear a few days after giving birth. Then the woman has irregular fever attacks with chills and heat. I have seen and heard it from John, and the women in the parish. The new mother has no resistance anymore then. She can shake violently day and night and talk pure nonsense. Hall is frequently called in. Then he usually gives as soon as possible a good prepared decoction of hartshorn in boiled rainwater. The woman should be helped when drinking, because she herself can no longer hold down her hand. Then Hall gives the same decoction, but with two fluid ounces of red poppies and an ounce of rose water. Often the woman restores well, thank God, he says, and that puts my mind at ease.

But afraid about being able to do it, giving birth that is, that's me too. If only the child comes through all right. And then Hall will say: 'All women can. All England has come through. You can pray, Susanna, I will also pray. And your health you need to leave to God.

Believe me, nature shows you the way. It actually goes as a matter of course, although you still must make a huge effort. You are strong. You can do it. Take the labor pains into account, strong pains. But the delivery will sweeten everything. And the midwife has already helped so many into the world, how about her? And if I can and may, I'll be there'.

But I am so ashamed, Hall, to have to sit or lie down like that. I must not think about it. You'd better not come then. No, please, do.

'Wife, you came into the world the same way. Believe me, you will only want one thing: that it comes out. Even if you were to be straddle-legged upside down. Have faith and trust, Susanna.'

This helps. Actually I know it all. I will be strong and everything will be all right.

# IX
# OUR ACHILLES HEEL

You know when the time comes. So this is it. It stretches your muscles and flesh, in a spot where that's never happened. So these are contractions. At first you don't know you are having them. But soon you will know them well. It is a diffuse, indefinite, overwhelming raw feeling of pain, and it is everywhere. Not only in the abdomen. It is coming on like the surf of the sea, forms a high wave, washes over you and ebbs away. Then it comes back again with the same strength, or even worse. You have to undergo this, whether you like it or not. It is the force of nature, primal force. Even though you have never seen the sea, then at least you know by hearsay, how the sea works. Giving life.

I'm so strong. I do not cry. I see Anne very vague at my knees. She was there all of a sudden, as mothers are, if you need them. She brought with her broth, caudle and beer, and lots of other things. Is grandmother Mary there also? And do I hear my John? It is not common for an expectant father to be present at childbirth. But he is, after all, a doctor. He is a bit used to it. He doesn't actually attend childbirth, though. That's for midwives, neighbors, wives, grandmothers and mothers. But there is nothing sensitive in travail.

They are shouting at me. Go on, go on. Carry on, carry on. Previously I would have found it embarrassing, to sit or lie down like this, but now only one thing counts. Let it come. Sigh, sigh, sigh, hours of sighs, and relax. Minutes seem hours. And hours seem days. I'm glad that Hall has warned that it will be painful. It just seemed dark outside, and then light and now dark again. There is no end to it. The pain comes, the pain goes. I'm not sure I will keep up, but I have to, I will. Sigh, sigh, sigh, sigh, but now they call something else. Push, push, push, go ahead, go ahead, go ahead. This is better. Now I can act for myself. Now I can really do something. And I shall push for the little scion with all power that is left in me. Relax, and again push. My body rips up and my head is about to crack. Relax, and again: go on, go on, go on. And yes, yes, yes, yes, yes, yes: there is your child. Our little miracle, our ... girl! John and I have a daughter. Shakespeare and Anne have a granddaughter. And her name is Elizabeth. And we call her Eliza. How beautiful she is! Every part of her sweet little body is becoming. Is there any resemblance to anyone? I couldn't tell yet. Everywhere is skin grease and blood. Such a slippery creature. And how she screams. What a throat! A shrill nightingale she is. John, you are a father! Father of a daughter. I cannot give you a nicer gift. Or should it have been a son?

What a relief, that mother is here. Everything is taken care of. I got the childbed linen from her. For me: beautiful skirts, fomentations, embroidered towels and bodices, which you can open from the front. For the little one: tiny bonnets and diapers and bellybands and small waistcoats and wipes, lots of wipes. And new bedding, because what a mess it makes: mucus, blood and feces, and amniotic fluid as well as wound fluid.

The big hearth is burning away anyhow this winter. It gives warmth and at the same time, there is a little bit of light. A little bit, because they say that, when the light is too bright, a confined woman could become insane. So it is. Comfortable - the shutters are closed, and Hall has ensured that all vent-holes in the house are shut, because the least draught will be bad for me and our child. Our beautiful linen is well warmed by the fire.

Where they will cut our umbilical cord there should be sprinkled a powder of resin and myrrh. On these two ends, at Eliza and with me, a piece of wool soaked in olive oil should be tied so that it keeps the powder well in place. The umbilical cord should be cut off three fingers thick from the belly. I am still connected to her whom I have cherished for almost nine months. Still for a very short moment... and then cut: separated forever. Go, my little angel. Your life is yours. You are now on your own and yourself now. And the first great adventure after your birth is: to be washed. They put you in a bath with hot water, milk and oil. And then your piece of umbilical cord is tethered tight against your tummy. How well they take care of you.

The firstborn of the doctor deserves extraordinary attention. They rub you in with oil of acorns, because that is so good against the cold or smoke. Now they wash you with cold water and your tiny little nostrils are cleaned with a finger. This is clearly less funny, I hear, and you turn all red. But you're still the most beautiful baby in Stratford and the whole of England. A little oil on the eyes, and watch out for too much cold and too much heat. They massage your belly and your bum, to let the first stool come out. And oh, my sweetheart, how tightly you are swaddled. That is good. So you will feel just as protected as in my belly. It should be done with care, otherwise you grow crooked, and you sure should be as straight-limbed as possible. There are enough children who stay deformed for the rest of their lives. A soft tiny bonnet on your head, with a warm compress in it, against bumps and against draughts. How beautifully that suits you. You are ready for the big journey into life. They will whisper, that you wanted to come quickly, thirty seven weeks after the marriage, but no one will ask questions. Children come often somewhat earlier and an engagement is also regarded as a pledge of allegiance.

It is not easy for me now that the placenta must be expelled. They press on my tormented body, and yes, here comes the afterbirth. Now I understand why that is called afterbirth. It seems as if it's a second delivery. Than oil on the belly, and a closing sheet swathed tight around it. All is well, now little Eliza is here. And how familiar she already is. As if she has been around forever.

She may not yet be breastfed. She first gets thin water gruel, currants and cranberry juice, because the first breast milk is not yet good enough, they say. And I have to stay in for forty days. What a luxury, but also difficult. John may not sleep with me now, because it's my purification period. I will miss him, but it will also be an unforgettable time.

Unfortunately I am not allowed to participate in the baptism ceremony, but they will manage without me. February is a lovely month to be baptized, the month of sowing and harrowing. To be exact on the twenty first of February of the year sixteen hundred and eight our child will for the first time of her life be carried into church, to the baptismal font. Will she be sweet or will she cry out loud? She will have a strong personality - you can see that already.

I seem to become spoiled at all sides. With many presents and with beer, which they pour for me. What a luxury. The only thing that I have to take care of is, not to get sick, says John. No fever. I was afraid and he's afraid of that. Giving birth is one thing, he said, but the time afterwards can bring so many problems. I do not believe that will happen. I feel so good and strong.

After forty-one days I will be allowed to go outside. For the first time as the mother of our daughter. If I see Shakespeare, then I am sure that he will shine as a grandfather. He will be intensely grateful and touched. How sad, that your father could not just live to see this, John. This is quite different from what you have experienced with all the other people and patients. This will make you strong and at the same time vulnerable for the rest of our lives. Our child will be our Achilles heel!

# X
# THE FOUR HUMORS

Around the birth of Eliza everything passed over me. Hall's work and the stories about the patients –they didn't impact on me anymore. After giving birth I still remained wobbly and emotional for months. Melancholic, says Hall, it's all in the game. But gradually, interest in other things came back again. I am glad he is thinking out loud again in my presence and involves me in the work.

According to strict Puritan views one should not gain too much knowledge. That could bring strange thoughts upon you. But in this I rather stick to what Hall and father say: everything a human being learns is put to account. And as the doctor's wife I still have to stay informed.

I am taken up by that melancholy. It is one of our four body fluids or humors which determine the condition of us people, Hall told me. If a certain moisture is extra present in you, this may determine your character, and then it exists in your features too. You are more susceptible to some diseases than others. And you can best be cured with natural preparations that are opposite to the moisture which prevails. So for example, to combat the dry melancholy it is best to use damp means, and against an excess of wet body fluids, such as phlegm and blood, you use a dry medication.

Of course, I knew from grandmother and mother just about how it was, but when I want to pass it on to Eliza later on, without leaning on Hall, I must be more exact.

Melancholic John called me, but then again slightly melancholic, I hope, and that just temporarily, after giving birth. Melancholy is the best known humor or temperament, according to doctor Hippocrates.

Then you have too much black bile. Galen, who was after him the most famous doctor of antiquity, said that black bile is dried blood. That melancholic people often have pain in their stomach. That they think deeply and are frequently rather depressed, as you can see with philosophers and artists. I'm not a philosopher and not an artist, but yet I know a little bit how it feels since giving birth. The budding green outside was suddenly not so green anymore, actually even gray. Fortunately that came around again soon and I could enjoy our little one as much as I could.

Those four humors belong to certain parts of the body: the black bile to the stomach and also to the spleen, the phlegm especially to the brain, the blood to the heart and red bile to the liver. Or is the latter yellow bile - I still mix that up. In any case you stay healthy with a balanced quantity of each. But if there is too much of one humor, or too little of everything, then your health is in danger, and you can easily become slightly or seriously ill and, for example, display different forms of fever.

The choleric person with his or her hot temper has an abundance of red bile. Or yellow - let's ask John. This bile is hot and dry, visible as foam on the blood, which is bright red and bubbles. The pure choleric has a reddish face, is short of breath and has an irascible character. I think this holds true for the aggressive Sir Edward Greville, who wipes the floor with ordinary citizens and always has his own way.

The phlegmatic person has too much phlegm, produced by the phlegm gland. This phlegm is immature blood, says Hall, and it's not easy to specify in which other places it is in the body. If someone does not have enough blood, this moisture fills up the gap. Because of this the flegmatic person is pale, slow and cool of temperament. I am thinking of little George Quiney, who is now eight years and has had to lose his father Richard at the age of two. He is really such a quiet and restrained little man. One always sees him think hard before he does or asks something. Would he even resemble the melancholic already?

The sanguine person has according to Galen the only completely natural humor, red and sweet blood. The other three types of humor are derivatives of this one. That is why this person is generally healthy and strong, and he or she will be compared with childhood and with spring and air. He or she is the one though who acts first and thinks only later. Our Queen Elizabeth was thus powerful and healthy, but with her far-reaching intelligence she perhaps belonged to the phlegmatic type too. She always reflected before she acted.

This is what we humans are subject to. Above the moon everything is the same forever and underneath we, paltry creatures, are dependent on these temperaments and an uncertain temporality. I too would like to look at the position of the stars myself sometimes. So many people do that in Stratford, including our neighbors. Then the choleric is associated with planet Mars, the phlegmatic with Venus, the melancholic with Saturn and the sanguine person with Jupiter. But John will not hear of it. That has to do with that astral obsession of his father. That is old fashioned, says John. That is old hat. An old fight too, I know. Matthew Morris still keeps the books of father-in-law loyally and he knows that he will never actually have to give them to John. Whether he was really a doctor, old Hall, I don't know. In any case he regarded himself as such. He was a know-it-all and a difficult person, says John. He could be dictatorial. He wanted John to become a doctor, but then he was also jealous of his acquired knowledge. So you could basically never do well in his view. But I must not talk like this. Please forgive me. I must speak well of the dead.

My Hall has studied as to how he can best be able to practice medicine. In addition, he has learned by keeping himself practiced in determining from the urine of the people, what is wrong with their health. At first he takes a close look at the color of the liquid, by holding the bottle up to the light. He also smells it, which can make a lot clear to him. And he tastes the stuff too. I find this so skilful and also a little bit creepy. Imagine, if he himself catches a disease. But he is always grumpy, when I say something like that, and curt: what do thou know about it, wife, did thou also study medicine? If he starts with 'thou' and 'wife', I immediately know that he is at it and I prefer to hold my tongue. Some topics are better evaded in a marriage. I don't always remember that in time. Then I have already blurted out, what my initial thoughts were. However, I've noticed that John also likes this on the quiet. Because of this I get to know you better, Suzy, he says, when in a mild temper. For example, when we have lain together...

Anyway, where were we? Then he takes the patient's pulse and shall so decide on the combination of herbs, which he thinks are best for healing. This he passes on to the apothecaries. If they are out of stock, they send for it on the market, or they order it abroad. They then prepare the stuff exactly as Hall wants, and this is then used as emetic or as a purge. Or there are ointments made of it, or compresses. With bloodletting he has really become much more cautious. That used to be applied much more often, but it's not the cure for all ailments, Hall finds.

'Cupping' he applies very occasionally, that is placing a glass over the skin of the affected part of the body. One has the dry method and the wet. With the wet the glass is placed over the carved flesh, so that in this way blood can drain. This is also a kind of bloodletting. He has recently applied the dry method to Anne Ward of Stratford. She had black evacuations, Hall told, both from the mouth and from the lower abdomen. Then she suffered the so-called rise, the swelling of the lungs. She could not speak, she breathed out with a noise. For an hour she lay like this, so they thought she was dead. When Hall was called in, he set a large cupping glass on the mouth of the abdomen. He had first heated this dome-shaped glass and then placed it tight over the skin. With cooling the glass a vacuum is produced, which rounds out the flesh below it. After this well considered emergency treatment, she started talking again immediately. And so on twice. She held in her mouth, all of the night after, our 'pectoral rolls', those are pills made of medicines against lung disorders, such as licorice and hyssop, mixed with sugar. These are manufactured 'secundum artem', which is according to the method of the apothecaries.

Afterwards she had enemas, which gave two stools the following day. Hall then prescribed the recipe that makes the balance of a woman's body recover: a sweetened purge of tamarind, half an ounce, three drachm of amber pills with roses and a scruple of cremortart. That is cream of tartar, a cooling gentle purge, and it smarts a bit. It had to be made into a pill with pearl tablets, which used to be called Manus Christi, the hand of Christ. It resulted in eight stools and she was healed.

The working procedures and the help of the apothecaries is usually cheapest for the people. The poor often go first to them for medical help. Although my John is also not expensive and sometimes helps for free, or in exchange for a few goods or foods. He is most of the time well rewarded by the rich in the area, or they assume that Hall is so impressed by their distinction, that they don't have to pay. But you don't get something for nothing. Of course, there are barber-surgeons too, who can cut off for example a leg, and can also shave people. They are not that expensive too and sometimes able, but the most reliable training is still enjoyed by doctors such as my Hall.

I find it all mighty interesting and I feel privileged that I may hear so much about people and about a profession which I did not learn myself. While I have already been allowed to experience many things of father's world, this also adds something very special to my humble life.

# XI
# SEPTEMBER 1608

It's already September, autumn month, threshing month. The seeds are beaten out of the ripe fruits of the field. The leaves are yellow and red and brown and green. When the sun shines, it's like a magic world. And when it rains, it remains just as beautiful outside, but sadder. Yesterday we buried father's mother, grandmother Mary. Father is now an orphan. His father, grandfather John, died exactly seven years earlier, also in September. Father is sad. He loved his parents very dearly. Mary Shakespeare Arden was a special woman.

Very different from the mother of Coriolanus, the Roman warlord in the homonymous play, dad just wrote. The mother, Volumnia, continues to dominate her adult son. She has raised her descendant very strictly. In the ailing mother-son relationship all that counts is that Coriolanus acts as she wishes. She likes to send him into battle with the words that the mother's breast is just as beautiful as a head wound in the fight. The pride and hubris that he has inherited from her will cost him dearly. The great strength of the uncompromising man becomes his great weakness. Banished from Rome, he joins the enemies of the city, the Volscians. Because his mother convinces him to spare Rome, Coriolanus is killed by the leader of the Volscians. The relentless pressure of the aristocratic woman is central in the play.

How can father write about such nasty characters so aptly, while he has experienced it so differently himself at home. Grandmother Mary came from a distinguished family too and she also radiated that, but without being arrogant. She was a warm and wise woman. She carried the family. When she was only seventeen, her father chose her as the youngest of eight sisters to be the executor of his will. Robert Arden was a wealthy gentleman farmer with nearly thirty-five hectares of land in Wilmcote and also some in Snitterfield. He also leased to Shakespeare's paternal grandfather, Richard. So both families knew each other and my grandfather, John, fell in love with my grandmother Mary. My Hall believes that she had the qualities that Hippocrates saw as indispensable virtues, namely friendliness, dignity, neatness and competence. She conducted father, when he was a baby back then, through the dangers of the plague. Otherwise he wouldn't have been here anymore. And then I too would not have existed. How strange, if you consider. I frequently see now the features of grandmother in our Eliza, who is half a year old already. More and more you can see whom our little darling will resemble. But maybe I want to see it that way, to hold on to Mary. And after all it holds good too. Eventually she lives on in us.

Cleaning up the leaves in the garden. That helps. I do like it. No, let me but do that, I say to the servants. It relaxes and helps you unwind. Through your tears you can just continue. The rhythm of the sweep is like music. You move in a cadence. And you're in the daylight and in the open air. That is so good for a human being, says Hall. He knows. He himself recuperates when visiting in the surrounding villages, on one of our horses. And when he comes back again, he has a healthy blush on his cheeks, however tired he may be after the consultations. All this crosses my mind when I sweep. I wipe away the wedding-veil of the summer from the paths, so they become visible again. Also at the front of the house, so that it is passable for the patients and the errand boys who bring the bottles with urine.

Yesterday the urine of Mister Powel was brought. So Hall is now off to Ludlow. Powel has an eye inflammation, called ophthalmia, and an ongoing outbreak of ulcers on his face, so that his whole face is excoriated and he cannot endure any light in his eyes. Hall has made him amber pills. For an eye ointment was taken prepared zinc oil, camphor and saffron, twelve grains of each. This should be bound together in a nice small patch, a little pouch, which should be hung in rose water and white wine. Then must be dropped three or four times a day two or three drops of it into the eyes. Also he had the decoction of sarsaparilla and guaiacum with him. The latter is also called 'lignum vitae', wood of life, that's the very hard wood of tropical American trees. Isn't the latter used against venereal diseases?

Hall has told me recently more about Hippocrates. The learned man lived more than two thousand years ago. He was the first one to make medicine scientific. He has drawn up those rules to which a doctor must adhere to practice his profession to a high standard. He thus set up that oath, that a doctor must swear at the beginning of his working life. Literally it begins like this: 'I swear by Apollo, the healer, Asclepius, Hygieia, Panaceia, and all the gods and goddesses…', and so on. That I find so funny. A nice idea. Then you had so many gods and goddesses, and now we have our one God, to whom we pray. And maybe a few spirits and ghosts, of which we still are a little afraid.

Hippocrates had such beautiful sayings about medicine: 'life is the physician of diseases.' And: 'life is short, the art is long, the opportunity fleeting, the experiment precarious, the judgment difficult.' Galenus, who lived up to the year 200 AD, was the court physician of three emperors. He said: 'confidence and hope do more good than medicines. The doctor is the servant of nature.' Galen emphasized that you had to keep everything as clean as possible, hygiene, and temperance in all things. He said that the best physician is also a philosopher. That the philosopher knows how to think, how to follow nature, and how to combine these. That you'd better conform to the yellow bile, so that you are compliant to your superiors, and must struggle against the black bile, the irascibility. And that the doctor should bring reconciliation between body and mind.

Examining the urine comes also from Galen. And to feel a person's pulse. How fast the pulse beats says something about the heart. And the state of the urine about the liver. Thus one gets the most important information. But then you must, once you are with the patient, also look at the face and his or her attitude. The respiration is also important and what he or she secretes from above or from below. Whether one has a headache, whether one is gloomy or cheerful, the overall presentation should be taken into account.

You see, now I'm thinking about completely different things. Thanks to the sweeping. Grandmother Mary would also have said: child, you have to go on, there are things much worse in life. You have to dedicate yourself to your obligations and your tasks, and you should enjoy it, you know. Particularly enjoy as long as you are young. Now my eyes get moist with tears already. I go but inside. Never will I forget her.

John also loved her very much, but he has no time to dwell on it a little longer. From August this year there has been a striking number of sick people and unfortunately of deaths. From May to July it was the smallpox epidemic with warm-weather-funerals of both children and adults, now it is the bubonic plague. It is a term that I don't even dare to pronounce. Our Eliza is still so small but I can hold on to the fact that this disease does not affect the youngest so much. And I do always fear for the health of my Hall, who is short of help. He always has to readjust, for instance, when during his work it suddenly comes to something like a prolapse of hemorrhoids. Mistress Wincol, chamber-maid of the countess of Northampton, suffered from it lately. She had pain during stools and constant rectal pressure, and things bulged out, so to say. Hall had a handful of chamomile and one and a half pound of sack infuse on hot coals during two hours. In it were double linen cloths soaked and the anus was fomented with it as hot as possible. Then Hall pushed back the hemorrhoids with the hand and she had to sit on a sponge, which was dipped in the same decoction. I don't even want to think how Hall proceeded, but the poor woman was thus cured of the ailment. And also Mister Powel of Ludlow, with his eye inflammation and ulcers, was healed within twenty days, beyond all expectations.

The year has, despite the horrid epidemics, conveniently ended all the same. Shakespeare has become a godfather again twice. So there are two more Williams on the world, of whom there can be never enough. In October, a child of alderman Henry Walker was named after father while our Thomas Greene and his Laetitia had called their William after him early in the year. That was also for mother so festive then in our New Place, where Thomas is a tenant with his family. Nothing more vivid than a baptism. New life brings new light, warmth, hope, joy and expectation. The house tingles again. I have a feeling that grandma Mary still watches and smiles...

# XII
# TEMPTATIONS

Initially I was beside myself. 'Hall, don't you see?' But I kept it to myself. I thought I had made a mistake. I also felt it was childish of me and I was embarrassed a little for my immature response. But when it happened again, when one of the ladies obtruded herself upon him again, then I felt uncomfortable. The ladies could push me over almost literally in my own home, pass by me and ignore me.

Afterwards, I saw that I had imagined nothing. That indeed it was a fact. That these women exclusively and preferably wanted to take first place with the doctor. Because a doctor - that fires the imagination. He is a kind of almighty. Forgive me the expression. He can heal and rescue one from the clutches of death. And in one way or another it plays a part that he may, yes must, touch people and on sensitive spots as well. Sometimes on the most intimate little spots. And then imagination flies on silken wings. That stirs them up, those who yearn and crave for a touch, skin on skin. Especially by a man.

Meanwhile, I know them through and through. The temptresses. Their piercing or just evasive looks. They find it difficult that Hall is married, that I am his wife. And that I am also in the house and walking around in the practice. They want attention for themselves. No, they even demand that. They are the perpetrators. And Hall, with his patience and professional knowledge, commitment and compassion, is the perfect victim. He becomes involved before he realizes it. This is because he takes a different view. He begins with a searching look, with regard to the symptoms and with the eternal desire to cure or alleviate wherever he can. And since these creatures are experienced to present themselves as totally innocent, and yes even endearing... Fill in the gaps yourself. Often they have bothered their family, their friends, their acquaintances, their neighbors already to the limit. All those people are sick and tired of it already and are trying to dodge the person. I recognize that pattern at the market. Then I see it happen that people make an effort to suddenly be busy with something else. So the nuisances are getting less and less response. But in the stock of doctors they try to tap a new source of listeners.

Hall has so much experience and recognizes peoples' behavioral patterns. But these, usually graceful, characters are refined. Then evil has already happened unnoticed. And you as a relief worker can no longer shake them off. Often they are sick merely in their imaginations. So I subsequently have doubts about 'very handsome' Elizabeth Boughton, who felt a tumor with the size of a pigeon egg in her throat. There is actually nothing wrong with them, but they still come up with all kinds of ailments. Clever is the doctor who realizes in time it is affectation. How do you deal with it in that case? Because such people may report right away to the higher authorities that you, as a doctor, failed in your duties. How will you manage then with your good behavior to maintain your licence? I should not think, let alone talk like this. On Sunday I will ask for forgiveness in church. But as a wife you see a lot, you can look at it from the outside. A woman knows other women. She speaks the same language. I can however warn Hall and sometimes it helps. He cares a lot about my opinion. But I am of course not always there. Especially never outside Stratford. That does not make it any easier.

Also, I know that they cannot help it, the complainers. They cannot change themselves. They are cursed with a boundless need to exhibit. Often they didn't receive much love in their younger years and they cannot live without this complaining behavior. Then they get bored and are caught in a deep melancholy. Smart is the fellow who gets them out of it again.

Hysteria has to do with it too, Hall says. That is a tricky concept. The 'hystera' is the uterus in Greek. So hysteria is also called the 'mother'. That is caused by evil vapors, which ascend from the stomach or womb, the uterus. Galen said that was so because of the attraction between different organs and the womb, like a magnet attracts iron. It is a typical female disease. Those bad vapors come from rotting menstrual blood. Then the woman is stuck with annoying symptoms like breathlessness, palpitations, flatulence, indigestion, spasms of the stomach and pain in the joints. These resemble the symptoms of scurvy, but with hysteria you also suffer from various mental disorders and you get no dark spots.

The woman can have attacks, where she screams and makes uncontrolled movements. Then Hall usually prescribes a mixture with hen's dung and the cordials, coral and bugloss. He applies a poultice, an 'emplastrum hystericum', to the lower abdomen. He gives against fainting fits a suppository with the sacred powder 'pulvis sanctus', including senna and tartar. He also lets the lady preferably smell the fume of burnt horse's hoof and other 'stinking things'. He sometimes directs the vapor to near the genitals. I would prefer not to make a further representation of it…

He has them inhale 'asafoetida' too, that's a weird name for an evil-smelling gum resin. This he applied lately to the Catholic Clare Peers from Alveston, when her melancholy changed into hysteria. He treated her with a pill, in which he had crushed in water the precious secretion of the civet cat, mixed with root of bryony. Then he let her inhale the smoke from the asafoetida at night. With this she was cured completely.

Applying an ointment with expensive musk, which is to be applied to the inside of the uterus is a very intimate process, bringing the womb sometimes back in its place. So Hall went recently to lady Archer. Her uterus was tilted, after which she got hysterical attacks, with convulsions in the face. Also she could no longer talk. After fumigation under her nose, she could stand up and speak again within a few minutes. She had beaver secretion, rue and peony against the convulsions and medicines with mugwort and bryony against the hysteria. Whether my Hall applied the ointment in and on the private parts with his own fingers, he has not told.

Maybe I'll have less difficulty with this later. I always want to look with compassion and at the same time also keep an eye on everything. It's all in the game with this profession to deal with it as well as possible. Precisely now father is writing a winter's tale about the ravages of jealousy. It is not as dramatic as in the tragedy Othello, where the suspicious Moor kills his innocent wife. No, in this new work they live happily ever after. Yet, in the first half of the play, the jealousy of King Leontes of Sicily seemingly leads to the death of his wife Hermione. The King thinks his wife is in love with and pregnant by his old friend King Polixenes of Bohemia. Leontes suspects incorrectly that their own daughter Perdita is an illegitimate child of their Bohemian guest. He orders the little one to be abandoned in the wilderness. The second half of the story plays sixteen years later. Prince Florizel, son of Polixenes, falls for the charm of the beautiful Perdita, who was raised in Bohemia as a shepherdess. After the initial objections of the Bohemian King, which made the couple run away to Sicily, love eventually overcomes everything: the young lovers get each other and the oldies become reconciled. Marriages are celebrated. The divine providence of the Oracle had predicted this already in the first part and the youths make the elderly look foolish with their display of power. King Leontes should be ashamed of his far-reaching jealousy.

So you see that it's not only in women, and actually I know that too. Such a play always sets you thinking. Patience, calm and understanding are things you have to muster. The appearance you give of this, works well on both sides. In doing so I give way to no one, unless I opt for it myself. And when I treat everyone with respect, it will mean that no one pushes me aside. So take it easy, Susanna.

How particular life is. Strange though. When you look back you can see this better. I have from the outset always helped where I can with the sick. I always urged Hall to pay attention as soon as possible to anyone who comes for help. Usually I have compassion for all people. That's what we are here for. That's what Hall became a doctor for. The patients come first. With perhaps the sole exception of our darling Eliza. Your own child may very occasionally come first. And if John really has no time for her, then at least in his head and his heart he has.

# XIII
# MELANCHOLY AT SAINT MICHAEL, 1610

Melancholy is a strange state of mind. There is not only the light form I had after I had Eliza. There are different kinds. You have an emotion after grief and mourning, as with Eleanor and Philip Rogers. They lost their daughter Margaret last year. Then nothing helps, no property such as their houses in High Street and Chapel Street. They were in deepest mourning, like father and mother after Hamnet. Rogers kept on working in their apothecary between his medicines, concoctions and beer. That distracted him. Hall could continue to call upon him. But of course you still could tell that it remains. Especially Eleanor will never be the same again. Body and mind go through quite a lot, she told. She described a strange and unfamiliar pain in her breasts and uterus in the beginning as unbearable. I still see anguish in her eyes.

Melancholy is also called black bile. If there is too much or too little of this dark stuff in a human being, the mind as well as the body is out of balance.

Today Hall was at Leonard Kempson in Church Street nearly opposite us, husband of Margaret, whom John had treated for a painful hollow tooth. My Hall admires the gentleman for his musicality. In his house one finds so many music books and musical instruments. For example, there is a zither, a recorder and another flute, and there are two virginals and violins. The sixty year old man was very depressed by melancholy, Hall said. You see that often with artistic people. He had a very high fever and was quite sleepy, with the result that he had no resistance against the disease.

As a medicine he had in the morning and in the evening an extensive preparation for vomiting and purging. The following was applied to the soles of the patient's feet: sliced radishes, sprinkled with vinegar and salt and this had to be renewed every third hour. This pushed back the vapors from the patient and so he slept much more quietly and without the fear that went with his melancholy. Furthermore, leeches were applied to the anus, after which eight fluid ounces of blood were sucked out. Also 'lapis bezoar' was used. Bezoarstone is a small stone out of the stomach of a goat from the mountainous region of Persia, which serves as an antidote. With this Kempson was well for five days, but fell again in a shaking fever. He once again had an enema. Thus he recovered, was dosed up with the physic and was cured beyond all expectations.

So you see that for serious melancholy, accompanied by anxiety and fever, there is definitely some help. I personally have no need for such a drastic treatment, and yet I feel dejected lately and far from cheerful. I do know for sure that this is because Laetitia and Thomas Greene are going to move from our New Place to St. Mary's. They go around Michaelmas, the feast day of Saint Michael at the end of September. True, it is around the corner and we will look each other up as much as possible, but still I'll miss the sweet couple in our house and the cheerful children's voices with it. Also for our Eliza it will be a lot quieter.

Sir Thomas esquire, who never will call himself so out loud, is entertaining company. Mum and dad are fond of him. As well as of cousin John, brother of Thomas, who is also a lawyer and together with Hall sometimes an authorized representative for the conducting of business. And Thomas and Hall are fellow administrators of two sizeable pieces of land and sometimes together overseers on wills.

With the upcoming extension of the family of the Greenes, they'd better live on their own, they thought. And that is very opportune, while father wants to work less in London and will be more often in Stratford. St. Mary's House is next to the fence of the graveyard at Trinity Church. Thomas and Laetitia are quite fond of the charming neat house, in such a distinctive location. They are looking forward to the beautiful young garden with the charming small orchard. The children will have more room to romp there, though they also need to be a little careful that they are not too familiar with the many beggars and ramblers at the wall along the Churchway.

Laetitia has her hands full with the family and the removal. How does she manage anyway. My hands are already full just with Eliza. She is now two and a half year old, she babbles incessantly, runs like the wind and touches everything if you're not careful. I have especially to keep her away from the apothecary jars and the mortars of John. In addition, we still have of course the practice at home, which requires increasing attention. In the meantime, we hope for a second sprig - that would be so lovely for Elizabeth, a little sister or brother. But so far we have not got there yet. At the Greenes that has been easier. Their first baby is baptized Anne, after mother. Their second child, a baby boy, unfortunately died young and was buried on the third of August sixteen hundred and six – such dates you don't forget. Laetitia received a lot of support from Anne. The bond between both sweet women was consolidated then. Their third child was again a son. He was baptized on the seventeenth of January sixteen hundred and eight, a few weeks before our Eliza. I am pleased he listens to the name William and father felt honored. Unfortunately he himself could not be present at the baptism, because he had to perform twice that day for the King in London and that always comes first.

Also Thomas himself has been very busy with a new charter for Stratford and in July this year he has been re-appointed as steward - administrator and city clerk. Fortunately his brother John has been elected to the council at the same time and he can deputize for him occasionally. According to that charter of Thomas the beautiful old part of Stratford, Old Town, with the church and the churchyard, lies within the municipal boundaries of our city. The ramblers there are now also under our town jurisdiction. The city constables will have their work cut out. But first one will ensure that the long wall is going to be repaired. The wall along the Churchway is nearly three hundred feet in length. In addition, father and Greene devote themselves to the repair of our major roads. That is definitely necessary, especially after the severe winters. If you want to have anything mended, you have to get on top of it. You can't just leave everything to fate, as father lets it happen in his latest play, Cymbeline. King Cymbeline listens to the wrong advisers, the evil Queen and her son Cloten. As a result, he wages war with Rome and he loses contact with his daughter Imogen and her husband Posthumus. Twenty years earlier Cymbeline had unjustly banned the guardian of his two sons together with those boys. Fate intervenes anew: Rome is defeated by the sons, Cymbeline sees his whole family again and pardons his enemies. The King is not a bad guy, acknowledges his errors and also the power of Providence. The latter solution is easier for the development of a play than having the plot rise from the characters, as in father's earlier plays. That requires a lot more thinking. For that process one should be young, resilient and energetic as a playwright. One day apparently you will have used up all your ammunition. In the latest plays by father benevolent fate delivers a fairy-tale 'happy ending'.

I wish in ordinary life that was but so. Then fate already brought father back to Stratford daily and we saw him more often. I should not say this out loud, as for most of the time it means that, just like last summer, the plague prevails again in London. Then the theatres there are all closed. The previous months they had performed Macbeth in the Globe, and now, as always, they had to swerve to the countryside. But once he could stay at home, he could take his time much more calmly for his play 'The Tempest', that he has in his mind. In it he compares the volatile sorcery of the old main character with his own artistry. Father actually works magic too - he brings characters to life for the duration of an afternoon or an evening. I am curious how this play will turn out soon on the stage. The father-daughter relationship is again very important. The elderly magician, who rules over a mysterious island, is called Prospero and his daughter Miranda. There will also be a sprite in the play and a beastlike slave, and eventually everything will be all right by means of an amorous encounter of Miranda with her prince.

How well would father be able to continue to work if he remained here. And then he would probably also have plenty of time to commit, together with uncle Thomas, to restoring the roads around Stratford and other local business. When Thomas Greene wants to make out a case for something, it will then happen for certain. Uncle is a special man, always full of good will and willing to offer his great expertise. His Laetitia is at least as nice and has an equal measure of common sense. I always feel their mutual love when I'm with them. Two people can love each other unconditionally and steadfastly. For me they are a great and dear example. Everyone would like it to be so, I think. With ourselves we come pretty close. Now I feel a little prickling behind my eyes.

# XIV
# SUMMER OF BAD LUCK, 1613

Bad luck took over, the summer of sixteen thirteen. Master Shakespeare was deeply affected. He had just had to bury in February his last brother, uncle Richard, after last year Uncle Gilbert, and the beautiful Globe burned down to the ground.

They were staging a new play 'All is True', about the reign of Henry VIII. Dad has written it in cooperation with John Fletcher, because this John had the hang of writing already, for the sake of the future of the company. How I would like to be in his shoes, but such a post unfortunately is not for women.

The play flatters King Henry, praising how he has paved the way in our country for Protestant liberties. And that England was chosen for that purpose by Providence. The final scene predicts the great virtues of the newborn future Queen Elizabeth, and confirms those of the King. It was performed with great pomp and circumstance. No expense was spared on the costumes and the decoration of the stage. King Henry would have a grand ball at the court of Cardinal Wolsey, and some guns had to go off, when his Majesty entered. The story goes that paper or other material singed and reached the thatched roof. At first one thought that it only gave a little bit of smoke, and one concentrated again on the performance. But inside the roofing apparently it began to glow, and in no time the fire was spreading and the entire building burst into flames. Imagine the panic that broke out. The theatre was filled up to the eaves with spectators. From the stage they tried to calm the people to leave the building patiently. There were only two exits, so a little caution was necessary. How successfully they handled it: there was only one man whose sleeves were burning, but someone had the presence of mind to quench that with beer. Afterwards, there remained only the sight of burned wood and straw and a few smouldering coats and hats. The proud stage of Burbage and father, Heminge, Condell and Armin the clown, burned to the ground. All had managed to bring themselves to safety. Only a few pieces of pillars were still standing.

But next year they will have it rebuilt. They want the building octagonal instead of circular. This time with roof tiles instead of inflammable thatch. They are right in this. And then they want to reopen it before Midsummer's day. I'm sure it will be a really wonderful theatre anew.

Normally I love this time of year. Everything blooming, everything green. The birds all busy. The people lightly dressed and merrier than usual. Then I myself am cheerful too and I'm now just thirty, a jubilee year. That feels festive.

I always like to go to the market on Thursday to go shopping. Meat on Rother Market and Sheep Street, haberdashery in Henley Street, wood and pewter in Wood Street, corn, salt and sugar here in Corn Street, our Chapel Street, white meat, butter, cheese, eggs and fruit at the White Cross and so on. You meet everyone there, both from Stratford itself as well as from the surrounding villages, because our city is the most central. South of us there are the wheat fields and to the north there is a lot of cattle. Those two mutually depend on each other and so it is always crowded here. This is also good for mother, with her malt trade. It is nice investment in addition and behind New Place we have two beautiful spacious barns for storage. If possible I like to lend a helping hand.

Every Thursday the farmers come to our Stratford, to trade their grain and their animals. Then right away they buy themselves clothes, shoes, tools and sugar. They often also visit the hairdresser and the tailor, as well as my Hall. Afterwards they usually go straight to the inn or the beer house. Everybody wants some refreshment and to have a chat. Everyone wants to exchange the latest gossip.

I always like the fuss, but this time it's different. It seems they are avoiding me. Or turn their back upon me. Conversation suddenly falls silent as I pass a group of women. Eyes turn away. Whispering, tittering, sniggering, chuckling. It does not feel all right. I haven't got my shopping yet. I must still buy some yarn, and kitchenware, but I think I'd rather go home...

At home I told my uncomfortable story to John. What could be the matter? He shrugged. He had little time, as always on market day. Just then Robert, our tailor, came running with a violent nosebleed. Hall immediately had small rolls made of cloth, that are dipped every year in March into fresh frogspawn and dried afterwards, and these were put in his nostrils. Strong ligatures were tied below the shoulders of the patient. The following plaster was spread upon linen and again and again applied cold to the forehead, temples and neck: two handfuls of burned and pulverized 'argil', white clay, mixed with one and a half pound wine vinegar, till it had the consistence to make a poultice out of it. And thus the bleeding stopped. That was a good thing too, because the man with the most significant occupation of the village could not afford blood polluting his precious fabric.

'Susanna, that happens quite often', Hall said later. 'It will blow over just like that. You should not immediately bring yourself home. If I could do that, I would stay at home every day. Next Thursday you go back to the market, just as at other times. You will see that everything will be back to normal.'

But it was not. The atmosphere seemed rather hostile. Even the market traders were very short with me. But I am always a good customer though. Back home Hall watched me pensively: 'I think I know', he said. 'A story goes the round of the village and that includes you, Susanna.'

But why didn't you tell me, John?

'I didn't want you to worry, and hoped the cloud would blow over, sweetheart. They say that you committed adultery with Rafe Smith, the hatter, in the home of John Palmer. That mistress Hall would have caught a venereal disease. John Lane junior has given this talk to the world. Your father's friend Robert Whatcott was listening when Lane was spreading that nonsense. John Lane, a whippersnapper of twenty-three years. That lazybones, who did not wish to finish his school, and did not get his degree at Oxford. Known for his lack of self-control, and alcohol abuse and who uses indecent language and is good for nothing. It will have to do with jealousy. The papist will sure find that we, as Puritans, are too successful in our Stratford. That we are doing too well in comparison with his own wearisome life. That can breed bad blood. I didn't want to say it to you, love. I was hoping that it would remain a storm in a teacup.'

You cannot have thought something of it, John. Rafe Smith, a married man, would you believe. And even if he was not married. I would never do such a thing in my life. Moreover, I cannot bear to think about it. God forbid!

'Of course not, dear, but at last it turns your head. Then your mind spins. Then I couldn't help thinking: maybe you are too amicable, when you console people. You are so open and extrovert. You empathize so with all people. You think along with them. You comfort them and throw your arms around all of Stratford. People can suddenly just imagine anything. And then I thought for a moment: am I not too long from home, when I visit my patients in the surroundings.'

Now you make me very sad, Hall. Now you have really hurt me. What do you think of me. I, who listen to all the stories. About lady Rainsford, whom you call so beautiful and shapely: 'formosa et optima structura'. And lady Jenkinson beautiful, pious and chaste: 'pulcra, pia, casta'. And so on. I understand a little Latin too, Hall. Then I sure know that you do use your eyes, doctor. Did you think I had no heart? Did you think that I am made of stone? Did you think that I can let it slide just like that? I practiced and practiced, to handle it in a professional and mature way. To have confidence in you and in your ethics and your oath of Hippocrates. In your experience and in your ascendancy with people and situations. And I succeeded. I had acquired peace. I didn't think about it anymore, or with a smile. And I felt so ripe and thoughtful. I really had made myself familiar with it. And I was pleased with myself and felt just like a woman. And now I am like a very small girl, who feels injured.

Hall went down on his knees, bathed my tear-stained cheeks and held me in his arms. He kissed me as tender as on our first wedding night.

'I'm sorry, Susanna. I love you so dearly. And never have I distrusted you. We will see to it at once. We will report that wretch. We will sue him for spreading lies and slander. Never forget how much I love you, Susanna.'

And I love you, John.

Endlessly I hesitated between reporting the man or not. I felt just like father's Hamlet, with his "to be or not to be". Did I have to act or not? If I left things as they were, maybe the people in the village would forget it sooner. If I didn't leave it, there would be a fuss about it, but then I did stand up for myself.

Anyway: on the twenty seventh of July we had John Lane junior sued at the Worcester court due to slander and he was excommunicated. The crazy thing is, that I immediately feel sorry for such a person, who has already made a mess of his life. But Hall says then: let it be and leave it at that, Susanna! That I know and that I rehearse and Lane is rightly convicted. Also my John knows how to distinguish between business and personal affairs, because at the same time, he is willing, together with our Thomas Greene, to act as trustee on a family property of the sick Richard Lane, of whom John Lane is a cousin. I think that is mature and generous of him, and I hope to get this far myself. I really want to keep our door, which is always open for everyone, still open for everyone.

# XV
# THE PRACTICE IN OUR HOME

I'll just stick to the nice things in life again. Our friend master Matthew Morris is getting married on the thirteenth of October to Elizabeth Rogers. Matthew is to John the link between his childhood and our new life here. Hall is fond of him. Those two can get along so well. Better than brothers. Half a word is enough.

Morris will marry Elizabeth, who is a cousin of Henry Walker, three times the bailiff of our city and a close friend of father. The mother of the bride, who is also called Elizabeth, is a sister of master Walker. Matthew is very well off with his fiancée. She is so charming, nice and sweet.

The house in Sheep Street, called 'the Shrieves House', where they will take up residence, has long since been in possession of her family. The beautiful building is so big, that a large part of it has always been used as a tavern and distillery by mother Elizabeth. If you stand in front of it, it does not seem so grand, but when you pass through the gate next to it then you can see how far it continues backwards. Through that path the vessels with the spirituous liquors go to and fro. Father Rogers, who has unfortunately been dead almost fourteen years already, knew how to handle it. He was known as a cheerful drinker. I am afraid the roguish fat man Falstaff in a few plays of father is very similar to the father of Elizabeth, but I will say this not out loud. Our former Queen was so fond of the amoral sir John Falstaff that she asked father to write more work with the corrupt fatty in it. After both plays about Henry IV and before Henry V father wrote The Merry Wives of Windsor, two ladies who take the funny knight in.

But to be honest: the bride and groom would have given anything for father Rogers to be still alive and present at the wedding. If only he could have known that one of his sweet daughters went to live in the beautiful building with such a suitable spouse. What a wonderful life they will have there, those two, and they are such a good match too. What a lucky thing that Matthew came to Stratford with my John then. Otherwise he never might have met Elizabeth. Our dear friends are welcome to all prosperity!

Meanwhile, there was also a fine development for ourselves. A formidable home had been waiting on us, and not even that far away from our loved ones. We have lived there now half a year, in the house of our dreams in Old Town Stratford. It is a tall and roomy home, made with strong oak and immaculate plastering. It has a solid stone foundation and a tiled roof with many gables and large chimneys. It is large enough for John's practice. And it has, very special, soft green stained-glass windows, as one of the few houses in Stratford. And spacious stables for the horses. If I walk the street, and go round the corner along the almshouses and the Guild Hall, I need only to cross Chapel Lane, and then I am at mother's and New Place. And when I walk the other way, then I can easily reach the Churchway and Trinity Church and I am a little bit closer to Laetitia and Thomas. Then Eliza can play yet again more frequently with the little Greene children. A house for ourselves, where we are with our own little family, and our own business. Where we can receive our guests, provided for by our own servants. Where I can run our household all by myself.

As you enter, you stand in the beautiful hall with on the right the large stone fireplace. On the left you see our parlor. On the right past the hearth is the wide staircase with the finely carved wooden bannisters. Behind it lies the roomy kitchen, overlooking the lovely deep garden. On the first floor there are the bedrooms. Ours and the one of Eliza, plus the sleeping quarters for the servants, and behind it you will find the landing with the small windows, which also looks out on the garden. It is the most wonderful walled-in garden you can imagine, with spices for the medications and the most particular and sweet-scented flowers and herbs to place and use in the rooms and the kitchen. I always find it such a cute sight, all those fresh bunches hanging upside down on their nails to dry.

The parlor is the most beautiful and largest room of the house, to entertain important guests or precious family. From there a few wooden steps go upwards and backwards, which open on to a passage, where also is space for the pharmacy. There are the pots, jars, mortars and herbal books, including, of course, the famous book by John Gerard. That is the first botanical book in England, printed in London, with beautiful woodcuts of the ordinary and most special plants. I too can endlessly turn over its leaves. In it there are exotic flowers and herbs from the New World and the Far East. New species include larkspur, passion-flowers and orange blossom. New vegetables are cucumbers, pumpkins and white carrot, the parsnip. Then there are the fruits like apricots, figs and peaches. And the three main scurvy medicines, brooklime, scurvy grass and watercress, which my Hall himself often applied already.

In that passage he can also receive the patients or their servants. Or he gives his many instructions for preparing the medications. He regularly speaks with our pharmacists Rogers and Court here. Rogers has his shop in High Street, nearly opposite mother. There he also sells stuff, coming from other countries, such as Venetian turpentine and Burgundy pitch. And he deals in a drug, they call tobacco, against which Richard Quiney was warned by Sturley. It comes from the new world and King James is also against it. It would be unhealthy, although it seems to be good for a headache. You can chew and smoke that stuff, and for that you need pipes too. Those he sells with it, long clay-pipes, which are flat at the bottom, because otherwise the tobacco would drop out when you put them on the table. And he also deals in ale. A real businessman you would say, but he has not learned to handle money well. He always is short of it, our Rogers. He very often bought a batch of malt from mother. And up to five times without paying. His debt had by now run up to forty shillings. He knows so well how to charm people easily. Shakespeare and Greene were not at home. It was decided to deliver no more malt to the defaulter. Even when father was home again after a visit to Oxford, Rogers was so bold to borrow another two shillings instead of paying. That's how he is, out for your money you should not be with him, but otherwise I do like him though. He has helped my doctor well again with medications this week.

Hall had in fact to rush headlong into Alveston to see mistress Lane, who had such a pain in her chest and difficulty breathing. The poor woman has just been widowed. Her Richard, for whom Hall acted as trustee together with Greene, was recently deceased. I can imagine that she was oppressed, partly due to the circumstances. Hall has attended her several days with pills and an expanded decoction. Afterwards, Hall said, you can hang in the latter the following: mashed cinnamon, sweet flag and cloves in a small fine bag. This is "excellent and worth gold", he said. Mistress Lane had to take a spoonful of it at a time, as many times as the difficult breathing required this and swallow the stuff little by little.

All those ingredients. You can imagine, what intoxicating scents there are in our house. It smells peculiar and strong in here. There is an odor that you cannot identify, but wherein you recognize all kinds of elements. Liquorice and aniseed, cinnamon and camphor, roses and sassafras, which is the dried bark of the root of an American tree of the laurel family. I'm so used to it by now, I would miss it if it wasn't so. And I love to listen to the deliberations of Hall and the apothecaries about the blends they have to prepare. About the picking of the herbs and plants from the gardens. On the quantities, and the things to include: the flowers, the leaves, the roots or stems. To use them freshly picked or in dried form. Cut or rammed down, mixed, sweetened or diluted with other drugs. The men are so careful and enthusiastic. They work hard and can always appeal to each other. They can bicker too. Then there is some disagreement about the efficacy of ingredients, or the tenability, and also whether a substance will be beneficial or just harmful in relation to certain diseases.

Hall believes that by his Cambridge time and later study he is the expert. And that, I think, will surely be so. He has, of course, in addition to his solid herbal knowledge studied and received clarification about the human body. He has learned with which symptoms he should do what and which treatments and medications work best. Training as an apothecary doesn't come up to the mark, he finds. Anyone who knows the slightest thing about a shop, and has a little knowledge of herbs, can pose as an apothecary. He can get very worked up about that. If he is in the vein for that tricky subject, he can turn completely red. But he only vents about that in front of me. That he should not say when they are present, otherwise they would no longer work for him, and he would miss them. And usually they agree. Then you hear them deliberating quite thoroughly. As Hall also does with fellow doctors. For example, with doctor Bowles, who lives opposite New Place and who advises and assists him regularly. It does often strike me as companionable, all that buzzing. If I hear them laugh between times, I know that it's all right on that day. John will later in the evening be in a good mood and feel a little relaxed. Then he is more accessible to Eliza and me, and accommodating.

Incidentally, I heard that mistress Lane shortly after the treatment however is deceased. So that is very soon after the death of her husband. To two people who have loved each other very much and really could not be apart from each other, this happens every so often, dying of love.

Do I love Hall? With all my heart and I look up to him, with admiration for his profession. Here I have a book from fifteen eighty two by Richard Jones. It states: "It is definitely the role of the husband to rule his household, and that of his wife to see his orders carried out, but a good marriage cannot be built without the consent of both partners". Jones believes that something like free choice is the foundation of marriage. And that a marriage only is comfortable in the satisfaction of fancy. So, you better fancy each other, or otherwise love cannot be enforced even with all the wealth of the world. And where one likes to see the other, many shortcomings are ironed out by the married couples. Well, I don't know if I can be so docile, but the rest sounds very plausible.

Love? Sometimes you have your doubts, when you've had words with each other. Every human being does though, I think. But when I hear him coming out of the consulting room, or coming home after a few days of consultations in the surroundings, then my heart leaps for joy. Then I do feel that I've missed him. One must also learn to feel what love is. You should always want to do your very best. And to give, always want to give. Then you notice time and again how much you love the other one and that something beautiful will come in return.

# XVI
# FIRE AND FIGHT

Shakespeare is quite satisfied with the new Globe. Indeed the theatre did become octagonal. And the whole of the roof was tiled. Fire is so frightening. In the same year, on Saturday the ninth of July sixteen hundred fourteen, there was also a huge fire in our Stratford. This was in the dry summer, after the life-long friend of father and mother, Judith Sadler, had died in March. Fifty-four houses, one after the other, caught fire and within two hours they had turned into smoldering ruins. Barns and stables went up in smoke too, as they were vulnerable by being used for the storage of corn, wood and hay. Yet it was a miracle that the whole city was not destroyed because the stiff wind was blowing full on it. New Place, thank God, remained standing.

The whole town was in a commotion. Hall has done what he could to take good care of the victims and bandage the wounds. Maybe burns are the most horrid injury that you can have. I myself was totally involved with helping people and consoling them. Inhabitants and neighbors supported each other where they could. At that time it was: no one for themselves, everyone for each other. Sharing shelter and bread goes without saying in those hours and days. In our house and in New Place we could receive many people, thank goodness.

A month and a half later – we just had buried on the twenty sixth of August the last sister of grandmother Shakespeare in Snitterfield – the fight broke out again over the farmlands in the area. This time it was affecting the land around the town of Welcombe near Stratford. Father too possesses land there and tithes, together with Thomas Greene. This brings in rather a lot of money: they pay fees themselves and then have a right to a tenth of the revenue of the land. Now, the young Thomas Combe wants to change the farmlands there into meadow-land, just as Sir Edward Greville wanted at the time of our marriage. Greville has, by the way, not succeeded in this and so my John and Shakespeare think that things won't take that course. But uncle Thomas Greene and all the Stratford Corporation are not so sure and are strongly against an enclosure of the farmlands. The price of grain will go up at once and on the many acres only a few shepherds will be needed, so that all previous farm workers will become unemployed.

I am sorry to say that father was buttered up by the brother of Thomas Combe, William, who was aged just twenty-eight. At the end of October the brat had agreed with father that he would receive compensation for his tithes and that enclosures could continue then. For convenience's sake they have also just signed with the name of uncle Greene…

That autumn father had to be in London and my John too. I make the trip with them in my mind. I then picture to myself where they are at that time. It takes three days on horseback from Stratford to London. They then usually spend the first night in Banbury and the second in Aylesbury. If necessary the freighter follows them with their luggage on a wagon. Then I imagine that on arrival at the inn they first transfer the horses to the stablemen, who will brush the noble animals, water and feed them. If it is frosty, which makes the roads hardened, the hoofs will need an extra shoeing. I reckon the gentlemen then have faggots brought to let light a fire in the fireplaces, freshen up and have a well-deserved dinner. After a good night's sleep they will breakfast with bread and beer and after having paid the account leave as soon as possible.

Father arrived on Wednesday the sixteenth of November and Greene visited him the next day 'to see him how he did'. They have discussed the issue comprehensively and Laetitia told me later on what her Thomas had written in his diary:

'And he (that's father) and Master Hall (my John) say they think there will be nothing done at all'. And that an alderman is meant to have heard from the sly Combe that there would not be any land fenced. But that had made uncle Greene all the more suspicious.

Back in Stratford again in early December Greene called in on William Combe. He knew that the stubborn young man had continued with his plans. In an extremely controlled and friendly manner, uncle asked him, on behalf of the Corporation, to stop it. Thereupon the man announced very rudely and arrogantly that he would go on with it, and when on the nineteenth of December no longer any frost was on the ground Combe had his workmen digging again. The Corporation then turned to the local judges and some gentlemen, including master Shakespeare and sir Henry Rainsford. Just before Christmas that year almost all aldermen and burgesses were present at the meeting of the Corporation and all put their signature on a letter to father. They have asked him to use his influence and to revise his opinion. Also uncle Greene has written to father extensively about the major disadvantages of the enclosures. I'm afraid that father paid too little attention on receiving the letters, especially since he has so many other concerns on his mind.

Shakespeare's 'King's Men' perform not that often anymore as they used to. They played only eight times last season. Prince Charles has his own company. The court no longer inspires. People grumble that there are performances at court every day, but that the quality declines. The public stays away. Father loses in this atmosphere his strength of mind to write good new plays. He is rather tired lately. Maybe that is why he has been wavering regarding William Combe. And just before Christmas it badly affected him that once again they had to bury a young actor, William Ostler.

Meanwhile, uncle Greene still is tirelessly busy with the interests of Stratford and Welcombe. A letter was written to a prominent supporter of Combe, relying on his Christian morals, that an enclosure would ruin Welcombe and that the 'curses and clamors' of the 'seven hundred poor which receive alms' there 'will be daily poured out to God' against Combe and his friends. Master Greene was so occupied with all this that he wrote in his diary that 'men live as though no death will follow'. At the end of December his Laetitia transformed these words into fact and gave birth to a healthy son, whom they named 'Thomas'.

In January of the new year it was bound to come to a fight: high on his horse sat a mockingly smiling William Combe. He encouraged his diggers to stand against those who tried to fill up the ditches. Among the latter was the brave foster son of Greene, Chandler. Before that, Combe called the Corporation names like 'factious knaves', 'Puritan knaves' and 'underlings in their colour' and declared he would do them 'all the mischief he could'.

At one point Combe realized that it wouldn't get him anywhere like this. He decided to go to St. Mary's House to suck up to uncle Greene. He asked him to prepare a peace proposal and wanted to seduce him with ten pound, so uncle could buy a gelding. But you sure didn't need to try that one on uncle. To make a long story short, the whole thing came up at the Court of Assizes that has mediated between the two sides.

Then uncle Greene got to hear for the first time, that father had signed an agreement last year with Combe and had given no more thought to it. I'm afraid this cooled down the relationship between uncle and his 'coz' Shakespeare somewhat. All the more so since suddenly it turned out that one had added for convenience the signature of uncle himself without his knowledge. That of course should never have been allowed to happen. Only when alderman Barber and his wife died four days one after the other, who also had been called names by the arrogant country-squire, father did wake up to it all. He finally expressed his disapproval openly of Combe and the enclosures in Welcombe. I feel a little ashamed that he came out with it that late. Uncle Greene had been in want of his support so badly, since the conflict started over and over again. The coarse Combe had seized the sheep and pigs of the poor citizens. He had let their harvests be trampled down. When people dared to offer resistance, he had them beaten and locked up.

Master Greene and the Supreme Court had wished to take measures against him, but it turned out to be already too late again. The brute had himself at the same time elected as 'High Sheriff' of the county, and remained in this way inviolable and untouchable. Were others yet again yielding to the one with the loudest mouth?

# XVII
# A THOUGHTLESS MARRIAGE

At the end of sixteen fifteen there were many deaths in Stratford. A violent epidemic struck in a stormy mild winter. The people slipped from Hall's grasp. In retrospect, I feel ashamed that he also rode to Shipston-on-Stour at my insistence. The young mistress Gardner of Shipston had a persistent ailment, leucorrhoea, also called 'the whites'. She was miserably weakened with it and deserved due attention too. I was happy for the noble lady that Hall was going there anyway. Such a secretion below can be quite annoying. By way of an exception, I was allowed to help with packing up his doctor's box. Hall had rapidly rattled off what was needed: freshly picked cassia, parsley water, turpentine, guaiacum. A plaster of ointment, gypsum and glair, as well as little tablets, made with coriander seeds, plantain and sorrel seeds. Red wine also had to come with it, because that works wonders with this disease. Hall told later that he was able to cure her well.

My busy husband had ensured that he could be back as soon as possible, to be able to cope with the epidemic. He had his hands full, it could but not blow over this time, but it decreased at some point, thank goodness, a bit. When the worst was seemingly over, we were in the first month already of the year sixteen sixteen and again in the middle of the preparations for a long-awaited marriage.

My little sister Judith is getting married. With her Thomas Quiney, who is a vintner and innkeeper. He is the fourth child of Richard Quiney, who really was a good friend of father.

Judith is crazy about Thomas, but master Shakespeare has his reservations. He knows too many innkeepers who cannot leave liquor alone, but he wants to give him the benefit of the doubt. Besides, one cannot stop a couple of lovers, not for the world.

I find it difficult that Judith is so touchy about us. The more favorable circumstances always seem to fall to me. That hurts a younger sister, who no longer wishes to be the tiny one. The early death of her twin brother pursued her like a shadow. Since then it seems she has lost her way. I also have a lot of grief over our Hamnet, but surely this is not the same. It is as if something lingers between us since, between Judith and me. What doesn't help is that father is clearly pleased, though, with my John. In this context, that feels uncomfortable, for all persons involved.

Anyway, she will get married. She is going to wed her fiancé who is four years younger. Father can make no objections to it. She is after all thirty-one. When master Shakespeare was aware of her intention, he sent for the executors of master Barber last September to New Place. He wanted to discuss with them if he did well in terms of last will and testament, and he let it rest for a while after that. A few months later, father's colleague, Robert Armin, the theatre clown died. On the thirtieth of November poor Robert was buried in St. Botolph's, Aldgate. Something like that rubs it in. Now father wanted his own last wishes put down on paper in January, while he still was 'in perfect health and memory' and his second daughter would be married soon.

Meanwhile, Thomas Quiney, the groom, would like to live somewhere more spacious, as he has but a small dwelling in High Street. William Chandler is prepared to exchange his large house, the 'Cage'. It is a distinguished and comfortable building on the corner of Bridge Street and High Street.

The public notice of marriage from the pulpit in Trinity Church was, as usual, put up already three times: on the seventh, the fourteenth and twenty-first of January. The wedding was scheduled for the end of the month. Before the twenty-eighth of course, since it then is Septuagesima, the third Sunday before Lent and that is the first day of the forbidden season for weddings. This normally lasts till the sixth of April, but now the two are determined to say Yes on Saturday, the tenth of February. So they will marry anyway during Lent when really no marriages should take place. They have also not bothered to obtain the necessary special permit. All right then. We'll see what will come of it.

We had hoped to hush up this omission. But Nixon from Bridge Town, beadle of the consistory court, let his tongue run away with him. He, who is not so very particular himself, who loves to take bribes to conceal someone's absence in church, who falsifies signatures and charges, was eager to report this. This was to be expected. As a result, Judith and Thomas were twice cited to the court of Worcester, but they had the nerve to stay away. Then they had to pay seven shillings in addition to the amount of the permit. They were also excommunicated for a short period.

In spite of all this, she was a radiant bride, our Judith. She sure is in love with her Thomas. He is also a particularly charming figure and a smooth talker. Maybe somewhat too smooth...

Rumors buzzed and after the celebration of the marriage they became stronger. Poor Judith. Another woman was said to be pregnant by her Thomas, Margaret Wheeler. Poor Margaret. In March, she died in childbirth and her baby with her.

The ecclesiastical court sentenced Thomas to three consecutive Sundays of penance which would mean having to appear in church in the white sheet, in front of all parishioners. That's what the adulterer wouldn't put up with. He preferred to pay a fine and confessed to the trouble in his own regular clothes.

Master Shakespeare and mother were furious and upset. Father had not yet signed the will. It was as if he had sensed it. Now he wanted to change the testament right away. His new son-in-Law had already failed to settle a promised hundred pound in land upon his wife and any children, what Shakespeare had wanted, and now this heart-rending shame on the family. Father radically modified his will in March. Of the three sheets, the first was deleted as a whole, and he had the second and third rectified. He wanted to ensure Judith had her own income for the future and drop Thomas, who had still not settled that hundred pound. He crossed out 'son-in-law' and substituted 'daughter Judith'...

I really used to fail to notice, but is it possible that there has always been between Judith and me something like displeasure, which culminated with her in jealousy? That you hear more between sisters and brothers. And now this is added to by the fact that John and I seem to be well endowed in the will of father, and Judith yet also, but much less. It might be common that for the most part it falls to the eldest, but this difference... I need to stop worrying about this, you'll get nowhere with it anyway. And I have to help Hall with the aftermath of the epidemic.

Of course the behavior of Thomas went down badly with father and mother. It was unforgivable. How could the wag do this to both women. He was already known as a rake and then to also impregnate another, with his own wedding in prospect. Dear Judith, how unlucky can one be. They say that some bring misfortune down on their own head.

# XVIII
# MASTER SHAKESPEARE DIES, APRIL 1616

How many people were there? Trinity Church was packed. I recognized from London friends and acquaintances who had sometimes visited us here. How fast it went suddenly with you. So you got sick and the next moment you were no longer there. My Hall cannot get over it that he has not been able to save you. Where was your resistance, father? You were always so strong. Have you taken so heavily to heart the misdemeanors of your second son-in-law? You, who got used to so many things in turbulent London. But when injustice affects your own child...

The moment when the coffin was carried inside I was moved to tears and then I could no longer remember whole parts of the ceremony. Apparently memory works like this – what you cannot bear gets temporarily or perhaps permanently deleted.

And now you lie here. Under a heavy stone. Dear master Shakespeare. Dear father. Dear bones. How a body does fare then - I don't even want to think about it. You have written yourself something about that in your Hamlet, when he sees how a grave-digger excavates the skull of Jorick, the court jester. He had been so dear to Crown Prince Hamlet. It's about the inevitability and acceptance of death. And what you had put on your own stone, I read over and over again:

*'Good Frend, for Iesus' sake forbeare,*
*To digg the dust enclosed heare:*
*Bleste be ye man yt spares thes stones,*
*And curst be he yt moves my bones.'*

So no one would ever dare to touch the stones of your grave and your bones. At night these lines go by through my head. Time and again, without end. Tiring. But I quieten down as I sit here, in the soothing coolness of the church. I like it best when I'm all alone.

Then it is as if I can talk with you. And I can too. You are still here for me. I know where your body is. Forever in one place. Never in London again or any other town, to perform or for business. Or else you were in Stratford, but then busy with a new play, or also with business, or having a lively time along with friends and colleagues. And sometimes somewhat quieter together with mistress Shakespeare. Mother is so silent and self-absorbed. You must respect her mourning, which goes above mine. Would that I could just talk to him, she sighed, and I would also really love to do that.

All the little presents that you ever brought with you for me from London or wherever you had played, I store up and press them sometimes to my heart or cheek. Boxes of grease-paint or a crazy hat or a small figure. If I touch it, I touch you. If I look at it, I look at you. Then I hear your voice. I know what you would say. Then my heart feels your presence and warmth. I feel there is a piece of you, no, you are completely with me. For ever with me. I will cherish everything to my last gasp. Until it is my time too.

Such a horrid stone. So heavy and cold. How deep beneath lies such a sweet body. It seems stuffy to me, but then you breathe no more. Could I but conjure you up. As in your plays. A loud trumpet, and then the grave opens. Father, will you play one more time for me. Just do something from the Tempest, one of your best plays. How is that scene at the end again? Where sorcerer Prospero in the fourth act says:

> '*Our revels now are ended. These our actors,*
> *As I foretold you, were all spirits, and*
> *Are melted into air, into thin air;*'

And then it continues further about how the workmanship of this vision, the towers, the palaces, the temples, the globe itself will dissolve and that nothing of it will remain:

> '*We are such stuff*
> *As dreams are made on, and our little life*
> *Is rounded with a sleep.*'

Beautiful, eh? And also depressing. On second thoughts: please, don't do that, father. Don't come out with this. I would break out in a cold sweat. Like Hamlet, when he becomes aware of the ghost of his father. You never know what you are capable of.

Your lessons in life and your wisdom. On paper and on stage they give consolation, for a lifetime. In reality we, your wife and daughters, were often made to miss you. Then we could sometimes grumble and be angry with you, in times of difficulty. We then immediately prayed for forgiveness. One needs to control oneself. But when you knocked on the door by surprise and suddenly stood in front of us, our life was filled with you. And with your cheerfulness and busy liveliness and also thoughtfulness and beautiful, special statements.

And now you are forever with us in Stratford. Your body now for sure is in one and the same place, but I preferred it was not so. Could you but still be in London, in the Globe. That I can imagine. In our daily life we got so used to it that you were far away, that I, even now sometimes, don't even miss you for a while. Then life seems as it always was, and at the same time it will never be the same anymore.

So often and long you were away from home. Hall is also frequently away when he needs to visit people outside Stratford, for example the count and countess of Northampton. Then he immediately attends their staff, if necessary. That may take a few days, the journey there and back not even counted. This too often makes me think of Anne. You, father, toured much longer if you had to play in London or in the other places. How on earth did she cope?

The nicest is the practice at home, when Hall is in and practices here. It really is very busy with all the people who come, but it also creates a vibrant feel in and around the house. Sometimes one knocks at the door at night too. Then the servant on duty first goes to see who is there, and what is going on. Usually Hall himself must come to them. At times he needs to visit a patient in the middle of the night. Often I myself am so privileged that I can sleep on. When I see him coming home later or in the morning, he can look so tired. And yet he must go immediately to work. But he always says that he gets energy from the people. That it is his calling and his destination and also that he is grateful that he has such a profession and, like his father, can do something for humanity.

More and more I am moved that I may live with someone like him. It is very special to be able to cure people. And I myself also have learned a lot. I can distinguish herbs and plants, and I can better organize now and got knowledge of mankind. In distress, you get to know the people. You have the attached and the detached, the childish and the independent, those who are nice and those who seem nice; the compliant and the troublemakers, the companions and the people who rather will be on their own. The aggressive and the tractable characters, people who are always hurried and those who slow down. The polite and the cheeky, the silent and the whining. Overall, I always sympathize with them all and enter into their feelings intensely. Sometimes too intensely, says Hall. With that I should become more professional, as he calls it.

I do find that difficult, especially when it concerns a child of dear friends. Thus, Hall last month attended Anne, eldest daughter of the Greenes, who is named after mother. The twelve year old sweetheart was suffering from a headache. Occasionally she got a vibrant color all over her body and was then white again. She was itchy all over, with virulent little blisters, so she could not walk without enduring a lot of pain. Hall has cured her with may-butter-ointment of elecampane roots and bryony, diluted with a little alum. As a result, she was clean and soft again. I was so happy for her and for her parents who could no longer bear to watch her suffering so much itching.

Soon we will move back into New Place, around the corner. You, father, have left us that large house, and also your parental home in Henley Street. There aunt Joan Hart, your dear sister, will for a symbolic one shilling per year continue to live. We had to bury her husband, uncle William, the hatter, a week before you. It is a good thing that we go and live with mother again, since Judith lives on her own. But one should not immediately move after the death of a loved one, Hall said. Don't pile up two major events in life. He saw too many people get deeply melancholic by doing that. So we will not go before next month. I hate removing. I will miss our house in Old Town so much. The beautiful practice, the lovely bedroom with the vaulted ceiling and the spacious kitchen. The dispensary with its pots and pitchers and jars and mortars must of course be transferred in its entirety.

But the garden, that you cannot transfer. That goes with you in your memory. With the picture of our tiny Eliza in it, who picks flowers and performs little plays. With you, her beloved grandfather, who watches her and quietly enjoys. Like you enjoyed me, when I used my girlish imagination and played for you. Especially when I had learned from you how to act invisibility. At that point one had to throw on a special cloak, so that the public knew: that is the 'robe for becoming invisible'. As a kid I was sometimes already allowed at your rehearsals, only if I was very quiet. Then I stood behind and in the wings at a performance. I stared my eyes out and drank the whole fest in. The grease-painting and the costumes. The boots and the wigs. The nervous saunter before one went on stage. The tensions and the little quarrels. The joy if it went well. The noise and the applause of the public.

It was busiest in the middle of the Globe. With the people who were not able to pay much and had to stand. Everything happened there. One ate and drank and chatted and screamed and jabbered and sang. Wonderful world. And also the world that kept you away from home. Actually, mother raised us almost by herself. That must have been hard-going, although you never heard her complain about it. But your influence was there though, father. We knew what you did. How hard you worked. And that you provided for our daily bread and butter. And that your work was more and more held in great respect. Even at the court, by the Queen and later by the King. When James I became King, your company was renamed the 'King's Players' or the 'King's Men'. You paraded, dressed in red robes, through London, at the accession of his Highness to the throne on the fourteenth of March sixteen hundred and four. Initially you played as many as twelve times a year for the King, what was allowed only four times for the old Queen. Until it decreased with this Majesty too.

As little one I played out everything with my own words and gestures, just as Eliza does now with such dedication. She is eight years old now. Will she still remember you later on? I hope so with all my heart.

But well, I can stay here no longer. I must get out of the church again and I must help Hall in his fight against the new fever epidemic. November last year, the Crown Prince, James' son Henry, died in London of it. His doctor wrote a treatise on this: 'Ad Febrem Purpuream', about the Purple Fever. That is a new disease that claims so many lives at the moment. In Stratford there are high death rates and also in the surrounding villages, Shottery, Luddington and Bishopton. It is important that we remain on our feet. I must be in daylight, breathe fresh air and must go on. Bye, dear father, I love you so.

# XIX
# A DIFFICULT CHRISTMAS

It is already Christmas. Last month, Richard Burbage, who unfortunately lost five or six children has been blessed with another son. He has baptized the boy William, after father, in St. Leonard's in Shoreditch in London. Burbage was and is Shakespeare's greatest actor. How that man can play: as Richard III, Hamlet, Othello and especially in the role of King Lear, he is unsurpassed. Burbage can do anything – he is also a good painter. He took pleasure in occasionally painting something together with father. For example, for the Earl of Rutland they have even manufactured an allegorical coat of arms. Father and Burbage had an intense unbreakable bond.

Just after baby William Burbage another dear baby was named after father. Our Judith gave birth to a son. On the twenty third of November they have baptized him Shakespeare Quiney. Oh, if only father could have lived to see him. So wonderful, two names of an old friendship joined together. It's been eight months since dad passed away. How fast things go. Eliza will be nine years old in February. She is already a little lady. She speaks sometimes about her granddad Shakespeare, but a child loses itself rapidly in play. And that's a good thing too. Such is life. I hear her singing through the house: 'The Twelve Days of Christmas'. Who has she learned that from? It is a wonderful song. Such a sweet melody, you sing along like that. But that may be sensitive, because it is actually a Catholic song. And Catholicism has been prohibited in our country for more than fifty years. Not everyone appreciates such a song. Especially not the most strict Puritans. They want to eliminate as many Catholic words as possible. In that they will not succeed. It is traditionally in the genes of our ancestors, and so it also remains a little in us. And some things are a sociable tradition and you really will never be able to banish those. You don't have to be as strict as that, I think. A little live and let live, that surely cannot hurt. Nice song. Twelve days are sung about, from Christmas Day to Epiphany evening: 'On the first day of Christmas, my true love sent to me: A partridge in a pear tree'. It is full of symbolism: with 'true love' you think right away it is your true sweetheart, but what is referred to is God. And the 'partridge' stands for Christ, who is in the pear tree trying to prevent the danger that can threaten his followers. 'On the second day of Christmas, my true love sent to me: Two turtle doves, And a partridge in a pear tree'. Those two doves represent the Old and the New Testament. And so it goes on with: 'Three French hens', which I find the most beautiful, because they represent faith, hope and love. This will run up to and including 'Twelve drummers drumming', those are the twelve points of the apostolic creed. It seems just a nice song, but it is composed to preserve the Catholic principles for young people.

Eliza chants it throughout the house, as uninhibitedly and beautifully as a child can sing. It warms your heart. She is so lively and playful. She is now used to us having moved to my childhood home, our beloved New Place. So we live with mother anew who intensely enjoys seeing her grandchild again each day.

For Hall and me it was not easy to leave Old Town. We had really had our own home there. Especially our garden we miss very much. Last autumn I went there to collect the final plants and herbs. Just let me do it, Hall, I had said. I'll pick the necessary ingredients though. I have so much sense now that I know exactly what it takes and how ripe or still young the plant has to be. It will still take a while before the garden here at New Place is adequately furnished and in order, at least if Hall still wants to grow the herbs himself. We'll see. It gave me the opportunity to say goodbye to our great pride. With my eyes half closed I sat in the mild autumn sun. That's the only thing that can really comfort you, the sun's rays on your face and then take a deep breath and let your mind go. It was September and there was still so much in bloom. All kinds of herbs and flowers. A cautious second bloom after clipping and pruning, or a first bloom for the later varieties. And there was still so much colour. Less bright than in summer, but still beautifully purple and pink and yellow. And then the red of the late roses. Woven in between the huge cobwebs of the gigantic cross spiders with their small prey. If it had been raining it always looked just like fine lace.

But I have to get to work on the preparations for Christmas. Several courses are on the menu: there is meat, venison, fish and poultry. There is much to prepare for. And the pies and the plum pudding should be ready early. They have to contain thirteen ingredients, for Jesus and the twelve apostles. Around the twenty fifth of December the plan is that all Christmas guests can stir the batter and mix. This from east to west in honor of the arrival of the three Kings. Their three spices: cinnamon, cloves and nutmeg must be in it. Each of the twelve following days we must eat a little piece of the pies, if you want it to bring luck. And the plum pudding is the dessert of Christmas dinner, with holly on top. Holly also brings happiness, for the men, and ivy for the women. Therefore I always want to have both in stock at Christmas time. And enough to drink should be there. Fine wines and beer, of which we must not drink too much of course. John will see to that. And an eggnog is a must-have. I always put a lot of eggs in it and some extra yolks. Then milk, vanilla with nutmeg and distilled wine. Serve cold, whisked cream with it and everyone is happy and cheerful. Finally the beautifully decorated sugar-work, on which I will work myself to the bone because our Eliza is so fond of it. The kitchen will be completely hazy and warmed up by all which is simmering and cooking. And above all by the large spit with the fat dripping meat that gets turned and twisted by the little helpers.

Our previous home was a real Christmas home and also here in New Place it can be quite cozy. But I'm not at my best this time. My brain won't work and my arms feel like lead. The other times it came very easily to me - to supervise the staff smoothly, to keep my balance and create atmosphere. Of course it is also a very different kitchen in here. I know it very well from my youth, but it must be managed properly and such a Christmas meal requires a lot. I carry through as best I can, if only for the others, though there is a veil of mist on it this year.

It distracts mother a bit, all the bustle, although her sweet head still is in no mood for festivities. She misses father so. At any time she imagines that she hears his footsteps. Those she still knows by heart. Smooth steps approaching the house. And then the characteristic knock at the door and immediately the most beautiful voice in the world. Father and husband was home for Christmas. Celebration time! Us children all going delirious and crazy!

Around this time he always had some performances here and there, but you could still expect every day, that he would just appear in front of you. That he would share in the conviviality and the Christmas rush and also go to church, if he could set himself free. Then everything felt safe and familiar. Everything fell into place. He also brought guests then with him, and he was so entertaining. Stories emerged from the previous year. What kind of things they all had experienced. At court and beyond. A whole world opened for you. Of play, fantasy and imagination, but also of the existing reality that was concealed in it. Then we sat and listened breathlessly as he got into his stride. While the darkness outside and the snow and the cold made you feel even more secure. Precious days, precious hours. How we will miss him this Christmas.

We write on the fourteenth of March sixteen seventeen. Hall is elected a burgess by the Stratford Corporation. He is not at all pleased by it. He has time and again explained them that he is much too busy for it as he for instance had to prove father's will at the register of the Archbishop of Canterbury in June. That is way up near St. Paul's in London. And then of course he has his hands full with so many patients, and the fever epidemic is still raging. Not to mention that he is summoned several times this year by baron Compton of Northampton.

This nobleman continuously suffers from severe toothache and swollen gums. First Hall has purged him well. Furthermore, he made a gargle in which a piece of sponge was dipped and applied to the painful gums. There it was held throughout the day. The second day the baron could eat meat already and the third day he was completely healed, Hall said. But he and I won't be surprised if it comes back, which is what one usually experiences with such complaints.

Hall has explained this case and more serious cases in detail to the Corporation. A leading man as the baron especially impresses them. They have stated that they understand these arguments of the doctor and that they will excuse him. Then he not even talks of a curious condition as that of the fourteen year old Richard Wilmore of Norton. The boy vomited black worms, one and a half inch long, with six feet and small red heads. His father came to our door with a few of these little critters in a piece of paper, which crawled like earwigs. He told us that his son was affected by it every new moon, unless he polished off as much meat that he almost burst. After treatment, the young man has never been troubled with it since.

We write on the eighth of May. We are not even halfway through the year and the family has to deal with a sore blow. The cute little Shakespeare Quiney died, less than half a year old. We will bury him in family circle. Fortunately, father won't have to go through this. Judith and Thomas are immensely sad. The only one with whom they seek comfort is mother Anne, who knows what it's like to have to yield to the earth a dear own child far too young. My John and I rather have to stand on the sidelines and offer no help. It's better this way. Everything wounds susceptibilities.

After Hall had refused to become burgess in Stratford, the Corporation has at the end of August decided to give that position to Thomas Quiney. Despite his less nice deeds they still wanted to entrust our brother-in-law with an honorable function. He can restore his reputation a bit with this and it will take their mind off things. Also it will afford Judith some consolation. Every little helps.

# XX
# SUSANNA AND LAETITIA: FAREWELL TO THE GREENES

Now they will leave us altogether. At Christmas Laetitia already hinted at it. Greene has intimated that they will depart this spring. There is no other town clerk to whom Stratford owes so much as to him. The Greenes say goodbye to Stratford to head for Bristol. Thomas wants to build up a new future. Laetitia has often told me how he worried himself to death about the opposition by the Combes. And that the death of Shakespeare has affected him so much that he was no longer able to keep his diary up to date for months. Father passed away in April and it was only on the fourth of September that the journal once more continued.

A month after father's death Greene got yet another defiant letter from Combe. Greene's stepson William Chandler received this at their fence. The bullying continued up to the end. Greene reports that Combe as a high public official still abuses his power by confiscating the cattle of the poor citizens and that Combe with his men lay in the ditches to just keep away other people's sheep from Welcombe Meadow. Greene came up with the advice to issue a summons against him to appear in the Supreme Court.

We will miss them at the meetings on holidays in New Place. But also just them dropping in or having a chat on the market, when we always compared notes about the growing up of the children together.

Their beloved house St. Mary's will be sold and also Greene's share in the tithes. The Combes are interested, of course, the money-grubbers, as if they have not enough already. That would clinch it for Laetitia. No stone would she grant them. Her Thomas has been so terribly annoyed by them. Always there was that struggle and the Combes were repeatedly prepared to risk hefty fines.

Greene's stepson Chandler has also had a run-in with them two years ago. About the enclosures too. William Chandler and his second wife live in Ely Street. He lost his first wife Elizabeth, the eldest of Richard Quiney's ten children, two years ago. He is a mercer and they are doing well, but they have no defence against such power-mad people. Now Combe's ditch is already thus long, that four or five hundred sheep are eating grass there all summer.

On the twenty-fourth of March sixteen seventeen Greene has given in his notice. The Corporation has made a bid for St. Mary's and the tithes, but Thomas rejected this at first. He would lose so much by it, said Laetitia, and they felt that he deserves better. Right they are. If there is one person who has devoted all of his time and energy to Stratford, it is uncle Greene. A few days later he was able to accept their bid, and also the Corporation was glad that the house didn't fall into the hands of the Combes. Laetitia is completely relieved. She had not been able to sleep for a long time. The idea that those awful people would go over her threshold and sleep under the roof, where she had spent so many happy hours, made her uneasy and sad.

Since they have left, we miss them and yet at the same time we are too busy for that. First there was the funeral of aunt Isabella Hathaway, the wife of the dear brother of mother, uncle Bartholomew. We have brought her from Hewlands farm in Shottery to her final resting place. My uncle is inconsolable. It is not quite clear to me of which disease she died, but it could well be that so-called 'new fever'. It is summer now and still there is the epidemic, with a burning malignant fever, an intense headache, all with severe heat, stomach ache and spots all over the body.

Ann, lady Beaufou of Emscote - Hall calls her "godly, honest" and of "a noble extract" - is also affected. She has those stains especially on her arms. Her urine was red and only little. She was healthy until the first of July and on the third Hall was called. Her belly was swollen and full of sick humors. Hall prescribed her nine drachm of our emetic. This gave twelve times vomiting without much difficulty. One could see that the noble lady because of the thirst had been drinking a lot of milk the day before. This was curdled in the vomit and she was almost choking. Then there came choler or yellow bile, with phlegm and burned melancholy, black bile. Stools she had too, six times, of phlegm with green bile and much wateriness. The vomiting stopped. After further treatment with laudanum, claret wine and gargle Hall gave her against the pox an ointment with regular oil and water of 'carduus benedictus'. This had to be shaken well, after which the distinguished lady had no scars.

Hall had to treat more and more people, who were covered with the spots and stains. The despair in such households is tangible. The sick cling to him with sweaty hands and bulging eyes. Hall then tries to stay extra calm to reassure them and to hold on as long as possible himself.

Meanwhile, the good news is that our Judith is pregnant again. We are so happy for her. They say the loss of a child can only be relieved by a new pregnancy. We pray that Judith may remain healthy and strong. Pregnant women should not catch a disease. They are so fragile and the unborn life with them is too. Sometimes my John saved them from a miscarriage, while often just after childbirth danger threatens because of a heavy loss of blood. Hall then quickly prescribes a drink with half a drachm shavings of hartshorn, to take in the morning for four days. The women usually feel relief soon and recover well.

We write on the third of February sixteen hundred eighteen. Greene will receive two hundred and forty pounds for his beloved house and for his tithes three hundred and sixty, in two payments. The money must first be raised via members of the council. Such a thing should always be paid on neutral ground. This time it will happen with us in New Place. It should be handed over to my John or to Francis Collins, the successor of Greene, or Greene himself officially. That always gives in a lot of extra bustle in our house. The rooms must be put in order for the reception, there should be plenty to eat and drink, and the servants must be well instructed which is something we are used to here. Our house is quite regularly the centre of Stratford.

The eventual acceptance of St. Mary's will be at Michaelmas, by the daughter of mistress Aspinall, wife of our schoolmaster. She is welcome to the dear home very much. The pew of Laetitia will be assigned to the wife of the Bailiff.

One week later, Richard Quiney, son of Judith and Thomas, was baptized in our Trinity Church. I wished Laetitia could have had a quick look at the cute little Richard. Judith did not dare to call him Shakespeare again, that would be tempting fate and a new little one should not replace another child. Dad would have been just as high-spirited towards his grandson, who is now named after his good friend. We hope and pray for a long life for the sweet little darling. And that Judith will be spared bleedings or other trouble. Fortunately, the venom of the fever epidemic, which has been called typhus again, had finally died down.

# XXI
# PURITAN TROUBLES

Sometimes I think that my Hall around sixteen hundred and eight would have preferred to travel to Holland too. There the strictest Puritans found freedom of religion. There they were initially made welcome. More welcome than in most of our England, where people who want to be extremely pure in doctrine are not liked. These are the people who want to get rid of any speck of Catholicism in the Anglican faith. Those emigrants it would seem are making plans now to sail through our southern ports to faraway America, to start again with a completely purified faith. In Dutch Amsterdam they didn't feel so much at home and in the more peaceful town of Leiden they are gradually also no longer accepted.

Recently it was so far so good in Stratford. Puritanism seemed to go down well here for a good while, but lately the atmosphere is grimmer. Catholics, Protestants and Puritans are tense and suspicious with and toward each other. It is a reflection of the war between Catholics and Protestants that has been raging for a year on the continent. Those tensions smoldered even under our Queen Elizabeth, who preferred to tread the golden mean. And yet she was at times very accommodating to the Puritans, then for a time much less so. After her death, King James stuck to the Protestant credentials, but one got more and more the impression that he wanted to be flexible towards Spain. And this has created bad blood again with regard to the anti-catholic people. And Catholic priests went into hiding, while their followers were, of course, enraged by that again. I abhor the story about a seminary priest who in the summer of the year sixteen hundred and four was executed by the agency of an extreme Puritan magistrate in Warwick. Even before the poor soul was dead, he was cut loose from the gallows. His stomach was torn open, his intestines were pulled out and he was beheaded and quartered. How much pain do people have to give each other for the sake of religion.

Now the atmosphere in our Stratford is so tense again. Catholic reverends have long since been deprived. The Protestant John Rogers has already been appointed in sixteen hundred and six, now already thirteen years ago, but he is a pluralist, so he allows multiple views to coexist. Dad could probably have appreciated that. They had known each other well as close neighbors. Rogers lives in the old Priest's House in the Chapel Quad, across the street opposite New Place.

Such balanced thinking makes most people uncertain. The Corporation has repeatedly pointed out to Rogers that he must take a clearer position, and given him another chance. He got a nice new gown from the council, made of good generously-cut fabric, trimmed with fur. But one demanded now that the reverend should adjust his behaviour on all points. In the end, this was not functioning, they concluded, and the Corporation would prefer to get rid of him as soon as possible. They stated that they wanted a better orator.

Hall has still treated Rogers. The poor man had inflamed and swollen tonsils and that you can't use when you have to preach. It must have been the tension. As a father of six little children of course he feared for his job. When Hall came to him, the vicar could hardly swallow or breathe and he had the feeling that he choked. Hall prescribed him a drink with figs, licorice, raisins and aniseeds. A warm poultice of hogs grease with green wormwood helped against the swelling. In one night he was healed and this recipe had already been proven a hundred times, Hall said.

Rogers was dismissed from his living this spring. Sir Francis Bacon, Lord Chancellor of England, had given permission to Stratford to have him replaced by Thomas Wilson of Evesham. Right away it was every man for himself. The followers of Rogers were so creative that they made up opprobrious songs about the other party. They have hung throughout Stratford signs with ironic texts. I only hope that won't get out of hand. My heart misses a beat.

My Hall can take such offence at it. He bids me often to calm down, but he himself can get extra zealous in these matters. Could he not just be somewhat more flexible? Now and then I tell him that, but as he gets older he becomes less pliable. Then I try to make some jokes about it: or else our Eliza would not know such nice Christmas carols, dear. And I recall to mind master Shakespeare. He was not so very particular. He had God, the gods or the sorcerers invoked, according to the best results for his plays. Besides he took care that he never really offended the incumbent Queen or King. It could literally have knocked his head off and that, of course, is never worth it. A man must not get himself into unnecessary trouble, and then you should not be immediately opportunistic. Call it common sense, love, and you won't sink. But no. We write on the year sixteen hundred and nineteen and my Hall is very short-tempered at the least little thing.

He is friends with Thomas Wilson, the eloquent minister with very stringent Puritan views. This makes the vicar not very popular with most parishioners, but he will definitely be designated as the successor of John Rogers. He appeals very much to my John. Although my husband doesn't agree with everything he says, he has so much feeling for his friend that he would go through fire for him.

This Wilson is a Master of Arts from Oxford and is indeed very eloquent. Rogers cannot yet beat him to that, but his followers have rolled up their sleeves. They have been for some time now sulky towards the church masters and the Corporation. Hall says that we can expect anything.

Now on the last day of May Wilson would be installed as new vicar in our church and the previous Sunday he would conduct the evening service. But the frantic crowd had thought of it otherwise. They had armed themselves to the teeth with swords, daggers and stones. Literally they were shouting: 'Hang him, kill him, pull out his throat, cut off his pockie and burnt members, let us hale him out of the church!' Imagine that being shouted at you. A person's life is not safe there. Wilson had for safety's sake fled into the chancel of the church, where father is buried – just think! – and the church doors were immediately closed.

But it went on. We were dead silent and petrified in the pews. We heard how they were trying to break in and how they were pounding on the walls and doors. When they even threw stones through the church windows, we were mortally afraid. We dared not move and held our breath. We waited for hours until the ringleaders were led slinking away.

Of course Wilson has still been inducted. Giving in to violence is the last thing you should do. My Hall felt very satisfied and combative when his friend read himself in, the following Sunday, June the sixth. Many were there, including widow Quiney, William Chandler, Richard Hathaway, schoolmaster Aspinall, the Bailiff and his aldermen.

A few days later they began to grumble to Hall that he had not taken great pains over the much-needed repairs to the church and that the church revenues should have been spent on that.

I myself had noticed it already for a while and I told John so. Especially the chancel looks downright shabby. All owners of the tithes, and thus also my Hall, need to do their best to ensure that our God's House will be repaired decently.

Hall is angry and I'm angry with Hall. How could he have neglected this so? The place, where father is buried and can be commemorated, deserves all possible attention anyway. I know my husband is very busy and that his head reels but this is pure neglect of your loved ones. Although he certainly sets not awkwardly beyond his work about business, about finances, about practical matters, he has always struggled with everything that distracts him from his patients.

A month later, the Corporation officially decided and recorded that money had to be forthcoming to keep the chancel of the church dry. After father's funeral one had already made plans to erect a wall monument for master Shakespeare. On this is engaged at work, in London, one Gheerart Janssen, son of a Dutch stonemason. Janssen has his workshop in Southwark near the Globe and has also made the beautiful tomb of the rich John Combe senior in our church. Dad's friends will keep an eye on it to be sure that the bust will bear enough resemblance to their dear colleague. The sculptor will do his utmost and it will still take up much time. In the meantime, they can begin by doing up our church. It was almost too late already and my Hall knows that well. He is actually always willing to contribute, but he is often not in the mood for it, with lots of other things on his mind. Though he is determined to give the church a beautiful pulpit and William Chandler will donate the wooden canopy above it.

Chandler has still ridden with townsman Daniel Baker to London to request a prosecution against young Combe. Thomas Greene had, as his final service to Stratford, set up a petition for this. He had described that Combe had depopulated the whole village of Welcombe and had bought up there three farms altogether. He had one of them pulled down and taken away the land of another. Only the scoundrel himself still had a large house there. He really couldn't care less. From London William Combe got a serious rebuke from the Council, signed by the Archbishop of Canterbury. He had to restore everything just so, as it once had been.

I always fantasize about how our lives would have been if Hall had wanted to go along with the Puritans to the mainland. That would have been just after our wedding and maybe we had Eliza then already. We would have lived in Holland in the city of Leiden. There the pilgrims live in cottages with at most two rooms. Their leader John Robinson has bought a property over there near a large church, the 'Pieterskerk', church of Peter, with a yard whereupon he had built for them twenty-one houses. The whole is called the 'Engelse of Groene Poort', the English or Green Close. They say the people sleep in so-called cupboard-beds, which are a type of cabinet in the wall with just a mattress in it, with little doors in front. There are pretty much three hundred of those pilgrims who also live further on in that city. They are a close-knit community, connected by their very strict views regarding faith, which for me personally would be difficult.

Then we would have had to leave our Stratford, and father and mother and all the people here. The rumors are getting about stronger that in the near future people from Leiden and England will cross the ocean to America to start all over again. I don't even want to think about it. Maybe the tension here has built up lately in terms of faith, but that will also come around again. Anyway, I could never leave Stratford. And if I want to have a break for a while, then a trip to London is good enough for me.

# XXII
# THE MAYPOLE AND THE MAYFLOWER

Meanwhile they have just dragged our Maypole. How is it possible with such a feature that is normally the centre of our spring festivities. I myself have the best memories of those events. Every year we went already before daybreak on the first of May with all the youngsters of our town to the countryside. We picked fresh flowers and flowering branches of the hawthorn and turned them into colorful garlands. Back in town, we adorned the houses with it and we put up the Maypoles. Those trunks that the young men had cut down were towed by oxen, who also wore bunches themselves on their horns.

Once set up, we let fragrant garlands hang down from the top of the Maypole. We then played and exercised around it in honor of the new awakening life. By the evening we had made a fire and there was dancing and drinking until into the night. Also there were imaginative plays about the heroic deeds of Robin Hood and his mates and of Saint George, patron saint of England, who saves the virgin from the dragon.

In the early morning we as young girls had washed our faces with the dew drops to get rid of our freckles. Than you hoped that you were chosen as the most beautiful girl and crowned May Queen. Our Eliza dreams already of it. She is eleven years old now. Delicate and fragile and a budding female. Beautiful and witty and wise. Forward in terms of intelligence, but also playful. She believes that the elves are in harness on such a great day. Together with me she sews little bells on her clothes, especially on the legs, so you hear a light clanging with every small dancing-step. That keeps evil ghosts and teasing goblins at a distance. And if she strings together really nice neck-chains of the whitish pink daisies then the less well-meaning elves stay away. Besides, with these sunny flowers on you are more likely to have children in the future, they say.

You see her enjoying spring, Eliza. She makes the most gracious garlands with the first tender harebells. The primroses are also beautiful, with which the children have made already in April their 'tossies', their tussocks of flowers. The vulnerable light lilac cuckoo-flowers also join in the game and the shining yellow buttercups. And of course, that prickly hawthorn again, as it provides firmness, covered with rags and ribbons to appease the airy sprites. Oh, that delicious first day of May, rebirth after the long wintery days. Which girlie doesn't dream of being May Queen?

Out of the question, finds Hall, not even when she is older. He calls it a pagan ritual with worshipping a tree, and then those unattended youngsters in such a forest...

But this year, sixteen hundred and nineteen, things really came to a head. This time they managed to let the Maypole be the butt of the disputes. The pole was erected near our former house in Old Town at the entrance to the churchyard. Normally it stands for merry-making and for relaxation. Hence, it is symbolic of the resistance against the strict Puritan views in the Rogers-Wilson conflict.

Each time the people put forward that King James is with them. His Majesty likes to take the Puritans to task. Last year around Whitsuntide his 'King's Book of Sports' appeared, with rules regarding sporting on Sunday. It would please the King, that is to say: it is laid down by law, 'that Papists and Puritans, if they were dissatisfied and would not conform, should leave the country; that people should be suffered, if they wished, after divine service, to enjoy themselves with dancing, archery, leaping, vaulting, and 'such harmless recreations', and that May-poles, May-games, Whitsun-ales, Morris dancing, and rush-bearing should be permitted.'

Thus the people felt supported and demonstrated against the strict puritan Wilson around the Maypole at the Churchway. The summer after Wilson's appointment the road-surveyors found it essential to repair the Churchway. The municipality decided afterwards that it would be better for the new pavement if the Maypole was placed a little further down. It would have to be moved before the autumn fair.

In the meantime, it remained tense in Stratford. There were still rioters in the church. Mid-September, the Bailiff and his deputy had the Maypole removed. They assured the people that they could feel free to re-erect it six yards further on, as agreed. People had been waiting for this. At least forty armed people put the pole back on the old place, raging and ranting.

My Hall and all magistrates of the town called the actions of the rioters very shameful. They presented a bill in Chancery to the Attorney-General against them, because of 'malicious, libellous and riotous behaviour'. Of course John Lane was amongst them. Where there is a riot, there you can find the drunkard. Rafe Smith, with whom I supposedly committed adultery, was involved. Vicar John Rogers also couldn't have restrained himself. William Nixon, the beadle who had reported our Judith and Thomas, had participated. The Catholic William Reynolds protested that he, residing at the Churchway, was prompted by the others, but actually had not wanted it. In William Hathaway, youngest half-brother of mother, my John was so sorely disappointed, that he wants to reconsider whether he still would like to include him in his will.

In mid-October the Corporation passed a resolution with regard to vicar Rogers, who was then still living in the vicarage. It was decided 'that Master Rogers shall have three pound more to that two pound which is lent him by Master Wilmore: for which sum he is to give his bond, and to give security for his avoiding out of his house within a week, and to deliver up peaceably possession to the Chamberlain'. A few days later Wilson was again called names by a few women and they were denounced by the church.

When Rogers had then finally caught his bands, the Corporation agreed to have the house done up. The floors would be repaired and the paneling replaced as well as possible.

That is only a palliative for Wilson. All tensions did not leave him untouched. He came up to Hall with eye trouble. Besides, his wife Anne is predisposed to hysteria and that has not improved in the present circumstances. This has also repercussions on Wilson himself. He suffers from a harmful humor in the eyes. Hall prescribed him amber pills, which gave him six stools the next day. On his forehead, the temples and behind the ears was applied a poultice made with Armenian ointment and on the eyes the whites of eggs, beaten up with rose water and mother's milk. Our special eye ointment was dripped into his eyes two to three times a day. What Hall noticed was that the man, a little while after use, tasted the flavor of 'sarcocol' on his palate, which is a gum resin from Arabia. Hall finds that an interesting fact and would like to do further research, about how this is possible. With these remedies, the pious man, thank God, was healed.

I am worried, by the way, whether our Eliza can forget about ever being May Queen now with the permission of her father. She probably is the first to feel that. She will be disappointed. Girls have their girls' dreams. But I think she will not start on about it anymore.

Fortunately, there is in this turbulent time also something positive to report. Our Judith is again pregnant and all troubles of the town passed over her. On January the twenty third of the new year sixteen hundred and twenty, their son Thomas was baptized. Hall and I are unmentionably happy that their little Richard has a new tiny brother.

This same year some of the most fanatical Puritans sailed to America from our southern port of Plymouth. Initially they departed on a small vessel, the Speedwell, though later a larger ship, the Mayflower, was a perfect godsend. Nice name, Mayflower, for a majestic three-master with a large curved bow and bellied sails. That smaller boat, with which one had crossed to England's South coast from the Dutch town of Delfshaven, had been equipped there with masts and sails which were too large. During the first yards in the direction of America, in rough weather on the high seas, the Speedwell had soon made water. The emigrants returned to England and dozens of them had already lost courage, partly due to the roaring and rumbling of the rude seamen. They allowed themselves to return to London and travel back to Leiden in the Low Countries from where they had just left.

The others, the go-getters, put trust in their faith and in the Mayflower. They have actually sailed to America. Stories trickle in how they set foot on shore and how they gained a foothold over there. How they are trying to seek a livelihood from scratch and that it certainly is not easy. Through illness and misfortune they have already lost half of the people. But also that they are little by little beginning to feel at home and are determined to proclaim and spread their faith.

For me it would be more than I can take. I find their views so rigid. You wouldn't get any fun out of it – you would not be able to celebrate anything and plays they won't allow at all. I understood that our Queen Elizabeth could hardly bear their narrow-mindedness. She was a glorious Queen, who did not want to restrict the pleasure of others and wanted to celebrate life to the full.

I myself will try to meet Hall's puritanical views, but I would like to be our old Queen with her 'golden mean'. Time and again I have very carefully in our family pleaded in favor of some more flexibility. I cannot deny my own nature. Lately that is more difficult, since John wants to support Wilson and is so kindly disposed towards the Puritan cause. Incidentally, we have heard how difficult life is in America in the harsh winter there. I no longer fantasize that my John could have sailed with them as a doctor on the Mayflower.

# XXIII
# AN OLD FRIENDSHIP AND AN ILL WIFE

Our head can be associated with the Moon, the liver with Jupiter and the spleen with Saturn. Just as the planets affect our harvests and the fate of the people, you can get sick or keep fit under the influence of the stars. But none of that counts for Hall. 'Since my son John wants to "have nothing to do with these things" ', his father said always loud and clear. My father-in-law was a believer in that field, as John calls it. There was no point in discussing with him and we rather left it at that.

Matthew Morris never brought it up again. Dear Matthew, we love him so. Also master Shakespeare was fond of him. And together with John Greene, who was father's solicitor, Matthew was two years after father's death appointed trustee to Shakespeare's Blackfriars gatehouse in London.

It's been almost nine years since Matthew married Elizabeth Rogers. Their first daughter, born in August fourteen sixteen, was named after me. Unfortunately the little darling wasn't allowed to stay alive long. I can simply not describe their and my grief...

Their second daughter was born in November two years later and was christened Susanna again. And their first son, with whom they were blessed in December sixteen twenty, was given the name John after my Hall. Is that true friendship or not? Fortunately they live nearby, so we can look up and help each other, if necessary. They consult Hall on behalf of their children and of themselves in case of illness. They are careful to come not too soon and not too often.

For me it feels so beneficent in my own home, that my own husband is our doctor. Also for our child and of course for me and himself. When we even think there is something wrong, we ask Hall. We do not have to go anywhere for advice, we do not run risks to be deceived by a quack, and we are reassured right away about small things.

Anyway, at first: we must wait until he is home. Then: until he has no more patients that day. Then: until the administration is done. Then: till the consultation with the apothecaries is finished. Then: until he has greeted us. Then: until he has eaten and is quite rested. And then: until there is nothing else on his mind. But if there is something going on with us, such as lately with me, then he will be here sooner than we can ask. I have written about it later:

We write: in spring sixteen twenty-two. I pull the sheets over my head and am not here. I had no mind to anything yesterday. Not to the household, not to the practice, not to the care of my husband and child, not to attention to mistress Shakespeare. I feel weary and worn. I want to do nothing, and let the world outside turn but without me. Take care of it yourself. Mistress Hall is not on duty. She can no longer handle the worries of all the people. Care now but for her.

What's your advice, Hall, you are my doctor. I surrender. Completely. Luckily I won't have to bring my water. Everything is here and stays here. That is simple and convenient.

But Hall, where are you now? Let but wait the countryside and your expensive customers. But it cannot actually be so. Don't want it either. I'll wait. My time is my own in the warm bed and the clammy sheets. Soothing sleep, let me sink away, I want nothing anymore. If only that pain would not come back again and again.

Between the shooting pains each time I fell asleep and then I had dreams of large swarms of black ravens with cawing owls. There were also elves and goblins. I ran on my bare feet on a lawn and in the middle I saw a fairy ring of mushrooms with small footsteps in between. Then suddenly appeared from all sides figurines dressed in green with red pointed caps. Above them flew white translucent little creatures. Some of the first had their thin feet going backwards, and had on their heads cornets and pointed ears. Both white and green figures began to tease me – they pushed me, pulled off my nightcap, tore my hair and tangled it. One moment the action shifted to our house and then they noticed the dispensary of John. They giggled and tittered and caressed the mortars and the polished jugs, after which they started hurling all the pots. When they finished throwing, they wanted to take me to their own world and exchange me for a faery changeling, as they called it. This was to strengthen their own people with the power and the fresh blood of a human child. I remember that I thought: that happens only to infants right before their baptism and to small children, but they were inexorable. Very noisy they were, they shouted and sang and made music on grass blades and flower stems, and they danced between the meadow touchwoods. Suddenly I hit upon the idea of turning my nightshirt inside out to repel them. And then I woke up drenched in sweat, with new stabs of pain.

Hall later told me that I had been wandering in my mind. He patiently explained how he treated me. I always want to hear, what he has undertaken. You are eager to learn, he says then. And I also remember all kinds of interesting details.

Colic attacks they were, Hall said. He had worried about me round my bedside. Then he had made two good purgatives. 'Diaphoenicum' and 'diacatholicum', plus a purgative powder, called 'Pulvis Rodolphi Holland laxitivus'. They were mixed with oil of rue and milk, in order to prepare an enema. When this was injected, I got two stools, but it didn't help much. The stabs of pain were somewhat softened, but continued. I was at my wits' end. I held my breath and lay perfectly still. I always do when I have a pain. If I calm down I feel that I can control myself better.

A second enema with hot sack brought, I beg your pardon, very much windiness and alleviation. As before, with the noble Earl of Northampton and his colic, Hall said. Against stomach and abdominal pain a poultice on the abdomen is normally used. Now, my clever and able man used a poultice, recommended by one Crato von Krafftheim. This man had studied in Wittenberg in the first half of the previous century, together with Luther. This physician had given up literature and theology to study medicine. He was held in great respect in the German town of Augsburg, where he had a large practice. Well, that poultice contained 'labdanum', a kind of resin from a shrub of Crete. My Hall also added to this prescription 'caranna', which is a tree resin imported from South America, and then the fragrant herb of roses and an oil of mace.

After that, I was dead tired, but relieved and fully freed from pain. How beneficent it was. All my senses opened and I heard the blackbird on the roof in the evening sun warble his highest song. Then I could surrender to the soft bedding and a heavy languid drowsiness. Everything felt snug and secure. I was under a good and loving doctor's care. I sank away in a beneficial and, I think, dreamless sleep.

Hall has been able to cure me in the midst of his overbooked program. In retrospect, I feel guilty, not that I was so sick, but that I have reacted unreasonably. I know he just overreaches himself. In addition to his medical work, he must still assist the vicar in church and keep the people in line and sometimes fine them. He has been able to say no to these additional functions for a long time, but the pressure on him is enormous. Besides, he was again elected burgess, but luckily he could excuse himself anew.

Actually, in this year sixteen twenty two, he had to appear before the Medical Committee that visited Stratford, for his re-registration. Every doctor has to appear there once in a while to renew his license. All medical rules are drawn up by the College of Physicians in London. Usually, the Archbishop and the diocese bishops grant permits to conduct a practice of medicine in our capital city and the respective provinces and municipalities. Then there is an Ecclesiastical Tribunal, a court for special criminal jurisdiction that may scold and prosecute doctors. That consists of the Bishop and mostly also the Dean, who are assisted by three or four excellent physicians and surgeons. In particular, the Archbishop of Canterbury is authorized to award a medical degree to the candidates. Furthermore, I know that my Hall is trying to stick to the wide list of medicines that are included in the London Pharmacopoeia. That is the only guide to medicines, which are officially examined and approved four years ago, on the authority of King James.

My husband can get excited again and again about such rules that do not hold for all those uneducated quacks and tooth drawers. They do just what they want with what they take into their bulbous heads. Yet he himself always goes faithfully to the Committee for re-registration.

But not this time. He could, to his regret and despair, really not disengage himself. Still he was pardoned and later obtained the necessary new permits as well. It had been force majeure, they understood. Perhaps he was just at that time at the bedside of his own wife. My darling husband. I feel so much loved.

# XXIV
# MOTHER ANNE IS DEAD

We write in August sixteen twenty-three. Over here mother is buried. Even in death she takes up a modest place. Under a small tombstone, between the wall of the church and the tomb of father. She would have liked to have been laid in the same grave as father, but no one dared to burn his fingers. This is because of that curse that is chiseled in his stone, addressed to the one who dares to move the bones of master Shakespeare.

Thus mistress Shakespeare is laid more than seven years later in a grave next to that of him. And I got the opportunity to write an epitaph for her:

> 'Breasts, O Mother, milk and life thou didst give:
> Woe is me! for so great a boon shall I give stones?
> How rather would I pray that the good Angel should move the stone,
> that, like Christ's body, thine image might come forth!
> But nought avail my prayers. Come speedily, O Christ!
> that my mother, though shut within this tomb,
> may rise again and seek the stars.'

My words are put in Latin, and that sounds much more beautiful and more concise:

> 'Ubera, tu mater, tu lac vitamque dedisti:
> Vae mihi: pro tan-to munere saxa dabo?
> Quam mallem amoueat lapidem bonus Angelus orem!
> Exeat, ut Christi corpus, imago tua.
> Sed nil vota valent; venias cito, Christe! resurget
> Clausa licet tumulo mater et astra petet.'

That is wonderful on such a stone. My writing on your grave, mother. Now I can imagine somewhat, how it must have been to master Shakespeare. To see his words in print and to hear them pronounced by the best actors on stage. Thoughts immortalized.

They are going to lead a life of their own. They will gain even more meaning than you gave them. How many times have I read them out gently, sitting in the cool church, at your gravestone. It feels like an honor that my words are chiseled in it and as deeply felt as your arms around me.

Now you lie next to master Shakespeare, mother, forever. How sweet was your desire to lie next to him all days of your life in your marriage bed. The second best bed, as the best was meant of course for the guests. But this bed that father specifically donated to you in his will was and is the most intimate and precious.

How often was he in London or on the road. You were our mother in so much. So much that it feels soft in my chest like one large radiating spot of warmth and security. I cherish the spoon with which you gave me food, the bowl out of which you gave me drink, the clothes you wore, the doorknob you touched. The little space you occupied, is present everywhere and sheltering me.

How I love to walk in your footsteps to Shottery. Every time a robin hops and flies with me. They say that such a small robin brings a message from above and that he, of any unburied dead bodies, covers the faces with flowers and leaves. You were always so fond of that spry little robber. I follow your steps between the meadows, under the trees along the brook to the house of your youth. There I go visiting our family or even prefer to just sit outside and look at the house and then I think of you. Then I can see you and how hard you have worked there. How you looked after hearth and home and animals every day. You were the eldest daughter, soon without a mother, with only a stepmother. That will not have been easy for you.

Where did you both meet, father and you? Never have I dared to ask where I was begotten, but it must have been here somewhere. My origin. Maybe that is why this spot attracts me so. You, twenty-six and father only eighteen. How was it, where was it – one doesn't ask.

I can already feel autumn coming. Clammy haze. Also behind my eyes. And it smells more spicy and sharp. There underneath the sloping thatched roof, you lay awake. You were the only one to know, lonely in the night, that those soft movements in your belly had to be coming from me. Who knows, that is why I compose myself here so easily. That I can breathe here so deeply and that everything becomes quiet. And at the same time, I shudder to think that event took place already forty years ago.

I need to go back home. To our New Place in Stratford. To our practice and our daughter. She will remember her grandmother, with whom we have lived for such a long period under one roof, for a long time to come. She was your apple of the eye, mother. Already she is fifteen and a half now, to be exact.

This morning Hall also had to stop by to see fifteen-year-old John Emes of Alcester. The poor lad is still troubled with bed-wetting. Eliza could hardly believe her ears but something like that occurs frequently, according to Hall. He prescribed the young man the dried small windpipe of a cock, which had to be made into powder. Mixed with 'crocus martis', which is iron oxide, this had to be eaten in a soft-boiled egg and so each morning. Eliza hopes that it has made a difference, because she feels sorry for the boy. Maybe a little attention to him is even in this case quite adequate.

In recent weeks, Hall regularly had to visit George Quiney, who is a brother of Judith's Thomas. Those two differ a lot. It's true they are both good at languages, but George is thoughtful and learned and Thomas unfortunately impulsive.

George took his degree in Oxford at Balliol College and wants to become vicar in our church. He is also an usher at the Grammar school. I could already see it in him when he was a little boy. Three years ago at Michaelmas he became curate here.

He has managed to ensure that the legal fees were collected and that those also would be spent on the restoration of the church. He and the then churchwardens presented the Bailiff and aldermen, master Combe and also my Hall, with responsibility for the continuous state of decay of the chancel. Hall was ashamed that things had come to this. That such a young man, who is the youngest son of one of the best friends of grandfather and father, had to call him to order. George apparently had made an impression and from that time forth, the notables devoted their energies to refurbishing the church.

Hall would still like to make up for that and help George, who is at the moment pretty sick. The poor young man has a painful cough with very much phlegm. He even coughs up chunks, has a slight fever, and is weakened. His urine is red without sediment. Hall has put him back on his feet with a purgative and compound honey water. His head had to be shaved, and a complex plaster with hot and dry medicines could be applied to it. Although the wise man is not wholly freed from the symptoms, he still revived a little bit.

If I don't get up now, I'll grow quite numb. Everyone should take care of one's health during the current epidemic of spotted fever. The fierce little robin is taking on as if he wants to warn me against that. Yes, yes, you're right. I must go back quickly to help Hall. When I left the house this morning, he also had to visit William Barnes, who had an eroding ulcer on his leg. Meanwhile Hall will be back again.

I'll just cast a glance at the cottage one more time. I could write a poem about it. That forms just in your head. Too bad I have no hornbook with me - then I would have written it down...

On my way I can recall to mind father's words in the fourth act of Cymbeline, when it is thought that the beautiful dear Imogeen is deceased. It is meant to be a song and goes like this:

> 'Fear no more the heat o' th' sun,
> Nor the furious winter's rages.
> Thou thy worldly task hast done,
> Home art gone and ta'en thy wages.
> Golden lads and girls all must,
> As chimney-sweepers, come to dust.'

And then something like that you won't have to worry anymore about tyrants or about clothes or food. Neither slander nor censure rash. And further:

> 'Quiet consummation have,
> And renownèd be thy grave.'

In the latter mother would not take much interest, that her grave would be renowned… Father's wonderful words. Along with your sadness you just find comfort in them and in his knowing that for sure there is nothing for it but to perish like every other human being. And that you won't have to make a great fuss about a thing anymore.

But grief takes time and for ourselves I hope that it will still last a little while…

# XXV
# SUSANNA IS ORPHANED AND SHAKESPEARE'S WORK COLLECTED

Since mother is no longer among us, it seems as if father died for a second time. One goes with the other. If one parent is still alive, the other still lives on a bit in her or him.

Been up all night. With a shock I realized that I cannot ask them anything anymore. Ever again. Before, everything went without saying. Mother was silent, and you knew their mutual secrets were kept inside her. An entire marriage. A particular life, like that of every human being, every couple is unique. I didn't ask and at the same time I knew all knowledge about them to be safe inside them. But now, now I cannot ask them anything, while of course it is precisely now that more and more questions flash upon me.

She has taken everything with her in her head, in her grave. Perhaps it's better this way. Children want to know more than necessary. Fortunately, I have read a lot of the writings of father, and also read it out to mother, in the evening when work was done. She liked his sonnets very much.

As if she wanted to say: of course we loved each other, however different we were. That doesn't always have to be pronounced, not verbally or in a will. What is obvious needs no extra words.

And then she had me read her dearest sonnet, while I suspected she knew it well by heart. Of this sonnet she knew for sure that it was written for her personally, because it is an allusion to her maiden name, Hathaway. Father describes in it she first said 'I hate' to him, but that she is later melted by his sensitiveness and then finally saves his life by having 'I hate' followed by 'away' and 'not you'. Many sweet and soft words are in it, which he attributes to her:

> 'Those lips that love's own hand did make
> Breathed forth the sound that said 'I hate'
> To me that languished for her sake;
> But when she saw my woeful state,
> Straight in her heart did mercy come,
> Chiding that tongue that ever sweet
> Was used in giving gentle doom,
> And taught it thus anew to greet:
> 'I hate' she altered with an end
> That followed it as gentle day
> Doth follow night who, like a fiend,
> From heaven to hell is flown away.
> 'I hate' from hate away she threw,
> And saved my life, saying 'not you.''

Now, seven years after father's death, I read and re-read his plays too. That works much better now, since they are collected and published in print. Such a pity that mother did not just live to see this. Then she would have experienced how many people wrote a laudatory foreword about father.

Father's friend and fellow writer, the satirist Ben Jonson, who often could be so sharp, now called Shakespeare 'Sweet swan of Avon' and wrote: 'He was not of an age, but for all time'. Those are also for me such comforting words.

The plays have been assembled by John Heminge and Henry Condell, colleagues of father at the Chamberlain's Men and the King's Men. They knew father so well that they dared to correct the manuscripts, where necessary, in his spirit. They would definitely have liked to ask father himself for advice, but as long as someone is alive, it doesn't seem so necessary...

Thirty-six plays are in it, his comedies, histories and tragedies, from The Two Gentlemen of Verona to The Tempest, with a few works he has written together with John Fletcher. What a precious work, this Folio Edition. A prepublication was already at the Stationer's Hall in November in London, where you can buy so many books, and customers are urged to do that especially with this work. Buy!

Master Shakespeare's works in print. How sharply he typified the monarchs in his dramas. He could understand the human soul and knew how to show the weaknesses of the powerful people of the earth and the dangers of corruption and to expose unscrupulous perversity.

Richard the Third was portrayed as the most ruthless character who, power-mad as he is, kills his brother, his little nephews and wife. He is the man who kills even more political opponents and who, with his shrewd tongue, comes up with a justification for it. He persuades Lady Anne, despite the fact that he is the murderer of her husband, to marry him as well. The lady predicts that he later will kill her too, which indeed will take place. And yet father got the audience that far into the logic of the brute. So one could consult oneself and wonder: where do I stand myself actually?

Unlike bad Richard father lets King Lear, who is in the beginning also a blinded ruler, evolve to become more compassionate. In a raging storm on the heathland Lear cares for the first time about the fate of others. How fond I am of that struggling King, when he gets lost on the desolate plain. Around his head he wears a wreath with weeds. Burdock, nettles and hemlock, cuckoo-flowers and darnel, the herbs that stifle our corn. They underline the confusion of the old man. When the eyes of the sovereign have been opened at the end and he has to surrender his favorite daughter Cordelia to death, the spectator cannot hold back his tears without difficulty.

The modest Cordelia - father lets so many female figures speak in his plays. Would he ever have thought of us, of mother and Judith and me? Then I hope that we did not serve as an example for Katherina, the tamed shrew. Surely that will not be the case with such a fierce bitch?

The Egyptian Queen could also lash out in his Antony and Cleopatra. He wrote that play just before Hall and I got married. We were no more a sweet Romeo and Juliet, although we were just as much in love. Father liked to describe a more mature couple for sure. You should not want to make a literal comparison with yourself.

How I did love all female figures, except of course Lady Macbeth, who, having her eye on the throne, incites her husband to assassinate King Duncan of Scotland. And that one murder is not all - her

Macbeth has been crazed, also by previous predictions of witches, and gets even more blood on his hands. Lady Macbeth asks the spirits to turn the milk in her breasts into bile, but in the long term cannot handle her own badness anymore.

There were also enough gentle ladies, and father did not make them brainless. They sure could reflect, and to many girls he gave wisdom. He also had some dress up as a man, like Rosalind in As You like it, Viola in Twelfth Night and Julia in The Two Gentlemen of Verona. Then you got a boy actor who had to play a girl or woman, and who then had to dress up again as a young man. All dressed up to hold the love of the other up to the light. To find out who loved whom most sincerely. The most frantic situations on the scene had the audience doubled up with laughter.

I think also right away back to the thick drunkard Falstaff, or the adorable craftsman Bottom in the Midsummer Night's Dream. The latter is so stupid that he brags that he is the best actor in a small play and gets transformed into a donkey. The honored spectators went absolutely mad and father was overjoyed that it was successful again, as he also intensely enjoyed it when his actors could get the people to sit and listen quiet as a mouse. Something for everyone, as you like it: an airy contrast to serious business and vice versa.

At last father left the world of theatre behind and returned to our beloved Stratford. With that I always think of The Tempest, with sorcerer Prospero. This master artist can rule things and people on his own island and let spirits adopt a different guise. By the end of the play he says to his air spirit Ariel: '*Be free and fare thou well*'. Prospero himself eventually leaves his fairyland behind and he goes on to occupy a prominent place in the ordinary society: '*Now my charms are all o'erthrown, (…)*'.

If only mother could have held the Folio Edition in her hands. If only she had been able to look at his monument that recently has been placed in the church, just above their two graves, on the wall.

Not that I find it a good resemblance - but you don't think that of your own father, I guess. It is made from his death mask, and then it's no longer your father. Yet Johnson has done his level best and it's a huge honor that master Shakespeare has a memorial bust and that it has been given such a prominent place in our beautiful church.

I read and reread father's work, hoping to get to know his views better. Much I know of him as my father, his love for us, his pride and warmth. But there still is so much to find out about him and his work. Also and above all about his plays. What he posits in one play, he veils in the other, according to the head of state or the spirit of the times.

To remain impartial as much as possible and yet to hold up a mirror, that's what he strived for. Whether it concerned religion or love, life in the countryside or in high society, the forest or the court. The court often stood for society with its stifling rules and laws, where one may be blinded by ingrained habit or lust for power. Than one had to spend a period in the woods or the wilderness, where one then became refined by nature and its regulating laws and harmony. Thus one had experienced 'rites of passage' to enter the next phase of his or her life. Then the characters could return to the world where they came from, with new insights.

To that end father used all motives of looking and seeing, of the eyes and vision, of the clear look and the glare. So with King Lear, or with the Duke and the young people in the Midsummer Night's Dream, in which, Puck, the minion of the King of the Elves Oberon, has to put magic ointment on the eyes of the characters, to teach them a lesson, to give them insight into true love.

I will keep reading, and maybe time will bring the intentions of father nearer. A nasty idea, that I can ask him nothing any more. I would now like to have once more an explanation from himself of all his plays. That, I have not thought of previously.

Such is life - it will not be sent. Though I can try to be somewhat more open towards Eliza. Our generation is more honest with the children. I must do my best, also because we have only one child.

# XXVI
# ELIZA ILL

Our child is ill. Maybe she shouldn't have departed to London with her father. Even before that, she was already not quite fit. And now she lies here in her bedroom, and there is something wrong with her neck. Then it is just as though I feel it myself. You would want to take over the pain of the dearest you know.

The spotted fever epidemic is not the case, but it sure is serious and I sense that from Hall. As bold as he otherwise always is, he is now no longer. Paralyzed. Suddenly he doesn't know what to do. He would prefer to leave her to me, but what do I know? The ordinary common-or-garden pains, yes. Lots and lots I learned from mother. Like all mothers of Stratford pass on their knowledge to their offspring. But this…

Hall noted it as follows in his observation XXXVI, if I remember well:

'Elizabeth Hall, my only daughter, was vexed with Tortura Oris, or the convulsion of the mouth.' Hall said he prescribed her ten purgative pills with aloes and the drastic bitterapple. She took five of these on the first day, which gave her seven stools; the next day she had five stools with the other five pills. He dabbed warm the side of her face with an electuary with up to sixty-four ingredients and with 'aqua vitae'. For her neck was used the so-called soldiers ointment, in which is turpentine and oil of earthworms, plus oil of bricks. The latter is also called 'philosopher's oil': bricks soaked in oil are mashed, after which they are heated to let the oil out again.

She got benefit from it, Hall said, as her monthly bleedings were obstructed. He purged her further with so-called stinking pills, in which was also amber and the edible fungus of the larch. She took five of it in the morning, with the size of peas and they gave her eight stools. The next day she took an eye-water, with which her period started well. Again John used our ophthalmic water, while he placed two or three drops of it in her eye. When her bleeding yet again stagnated, he gave her a complicated sweat decoction.

After application of this the old form of her sweet mouth and face restored. Sarsaparilla oil was not skipped, which above all served to anoint the neck. This all took place on the fifth of January sixteen twenty-four.

In early April she went on a trip to London, and on the way back, on the twenty-second of that month, she caught a cold, and got the same ailment on the other side of her face! Then it was on the left and now on the right side; and though she was heavily tormented by it, she was healed by God's blessings in sixteen days, with amber pills. But first the neck was given a warm fomentation, again with aqua vitae, in which were mixed nutmeg, cinnamon, cloves and pepper. She ate and eats regularly nutmeg. On the nostrils, and on top of the head was applied oil of amber. She chewed on the healthy side on the root of a herb of the aster family, 'pellitory of Spain', and was often purged with the pills. And so our poor darling was cured.

In the same year, May twenty-four, she suffered from an erratic fever. Sometimes she was hot and after a while sweating, then cold again, all within half an hour and thus she was tormented every day.

Anew no costs were spared. To anoint her spine an expensive elaborate medicine was made with lavender. It had to be applied to a hot place for several days. One hour after it was applied, all symptoms remitted daily, until she recovered. She was saved from death and deadly diseases, and our dearest was healthy again. God be praised and thanked and glorified.

She had had bad dreams during the fits of fever, like me then. She dreamed of small figurines, she told later, some very beautiful, yes gorgeous, and the others hairy, scabby and so ugly that she was afraid of them. She had thought: I have not eaten though the yellow primroses that make the invisible visible. And she was in her dream angry with herself, that she had left the four-leaf clover, with which she could have dislodged the ominous creatures. Child of her grandfather and her mother…

It's a wonder that I myself still remained calm. When I saw Hall hesitate, I felt a huge resignation coming over me. Two anxious parents at the bedside won't work at all. Confident that she would be alright, I prayed a lot and that calmed me down. I saw her suffer, but knew that our only child would not be taken from us.

I definitely said: not to go to London, not since she is not well. That busy city, full of dirt and scary diseases. Far too many people and animals: horses, dogs and rats, huddled together. So much so that every year the plague prevails. Then the theatres have to close when more than thirty dead people are numbered in a week. And that noise always going on. Day and night.

But she wanted to so badly and she went. Since childhood she's been full of it, of London. The city, where the night life is as intense as by day. Where there is always something to celebrate. Where you find on every corner market jugglers and quacks, who draw your teeth and have a cream everywhere for everything. Where music and song dispel your melancholy. Where certain women walk the streets with their cleavage. Where you can be thrown into the Tower for one small wrongdoing, but also where you can come away unharmed with unauthorized tomfoolery. Where people live so close together that the stench is sometimes unbearable, but the exuberance so much the greater. Where books are first released and where fabrics and clothes are more elegant than elsewhere and also more shabby on the other hand. Where the rattle of carts and the click-clack of hooves fill the streets throughout the day. Where you have such a wide variety of plays on the spacious courtyards of the Inns and in the theatres, that you don't know yet which one to choose.

She heard with red cheeks the thrilling stories of her grandfather about the city of cities. Grandmother Anne felt differently about that. Only later she had discovered that such a city, far from home, entailed temptations. That 'faithfulness until death do us part' seems too long for a man over there. And not just for one man, but enough about this…

How many patients he has seen this year, my doctor. For instance there was John Nason, barber in Stratford, who two years earlier had acquired the license from the Bishop of Worcester to be a barber-surgeon. Since then, of course, he was able to do a lot more in the medical field.

The man was just forty and suffered very severe stomach pains after eating, which also cut up roughly into the loins. Poor Nason could not sleep at night and got nasty symptoms of the yellow jaundice. His urine was yellow and red, with a yellowish foam on top.

Hall served him an ounce of his emetic and had a recipe prepared with horehound, hops, roots of bugloss and elecampane. Geese dung also came into it. After the treatment the good guy got again a healthy color and was cured within a few days.

Unfortunately, last autumn the barber-surgeon died, since there are so many deaths in Stratford. Father's dear friend Hamlet Sadler is also among them, who had been the widower for ten years of his beloved Judith. And in April, young George Quiney has died, who worked so hard for the restoration of our church. After he was treated by Hall, he got the same symptoms back later of the so-called 'tussies', tuberculosis. He was such a decent and talented man. He was very witty and well-read and so nice to deal with. We miss him.

Happily, our Eliza is again so strong and healthy, that she will be able to withstand the current epidemic. For her I'm not afraid, but in mother's nearby Shottery the epidemic claims several lives. This fall and winter seventeen people died already, among whom uncle Bartholomew Hathaway and William Richardson. Richardson's father, John, stood surety at the wedding vow of master Shakespeare, along with Fulke Sandells, who unfortunately went under too.

The widow of William Richardson, the Roman Catholic Elizabeth, is treated by Hall for flowing of her courses and the whites. Hall gave her a remedy to gain strength and frog-spawn to stop the flux. Against her melancholy she got water of snails. The woman wanted to be never again without those medicines, and was cured. In this way she could handle the death of her husband better.

Hall also had to afford consolation to Lady Penelope Sandys of Ombersley, Worcestershire. She lost her husband in the autumn of the previous year, and now this year she gave birth to their son. Hall was shortly thereafter called in by the poor lady because of her painfully swollen haemorrhoids. He prescribed her first poplar's ointment and then rubbed the scene of the calamity with egg yolks, well beaten with oil of roses, to which was added a little powdered saffron. This softened the hardness of the tumors, Hall said, and so the woman was cured from this pain and she could slightly better endure the mental pain.

Incidentally in that ointment there is the black poplar and also mandragora. That is the medicinal plant, which I find quite special as the roots resemble the forms of the human body. It is said that the plant contains narcotic forces, similar to those of opium. Thus I suspect that the noble woman, in addition to the guidance by Hall, could also draw strength from this at her bereavement.

My Hall had to take care of grieving people all autumn and winter and I had regained my strength to assist him in this, after our own darling had recovered.

The following year she went again to London, Eliza. It was so festive in the city, she told. Charles I was crowned King as the successor of King James. That she didn't want to miss, especially ever since Shakespeare disclosed to her in detail, how he and his colleagues had walked in the pageant for the previous King.

Of course she went, but unfortunately she came back again not so healthy. As a mother I had had to follow my intuition, but I find it so difficult, to say no to my little one, who is the sunshine of our life.

# XXVII
# ELIZA MARRIES

Eliza is getting married! Saturday the twenty second of April twenty-six she will marry master Thomas Nash. Sensitive as she is, that date will be her homage to the tenth anniversary of the death of her beloved grandfather. Her Thomas is the son of Anthony Nash of Welcombe, a gentleman farmer in Stratford, to whom Shakespeare bequeathed a memorial ring out of friendship. The old Nash was a witness in many business transactions of father and was overseer of a part of father's fields.

Thomas is his eldest son. He graduated as a lawyer from Lincoln's Inn in London. That's honorable, but he has not yet practiced, since he has become rich after the death of his father. He also possesses an inn here in Stratford, the Bear Inn in Bridge Street, which he inherited from his family. There, Hall treated people too, including a servant of father Nash. The man was tormented by jaundice, a nasty tertian fever. Hall was able to cure him well, even though the yellow discoloration was on his entire body. The Nash family was grateful to Hall, for how does one get another good servant in a hurry.

Eliza and Thomas are our closest neighbors. Thomas has, with his thirty-three years, nicely taken care of that. He knows how to brag about it – so modest he is about himself! He also wants a family coat of arms, with the spear of the Shakespeare family in it and the three talbots, with their massive jaws, of the coat of arms of the Halls. It seems to me that he wants a luxurious wedding with all the trimmings. With multiple groomsmen in front of the bride, with ribbons and rosemary tied to their sleeves, which have to be of the finest silk. I think he prefers that a precious bridal bowl is carried before her of silver and gold, covered with again a wide bunch of silk ribbons in all colors of the rainbow. All this surrounded with music and way too much wine and beer. Eliza is more a child of her father, rather modest.

Thus, Hall has just denied a knighthood in February, offered to him at the coronation of the King. He doesn't pride himself on such embellishment. He finds that the King pursues a drifting policy and is unclear with regard to religion. Last year, the King married according to the wishes of his father, the late King James, the Catholic princess Henrietta Maria of France. James would have liked to see in Europe the Protestant and Catholic forces united, so that the tensions with Spain did not always build up. And within the 'Church of England' he wanted a free rein for as many opinions as possible. If everyone then kept to a few basic principles, such as the supremacy of the King and the Episcopal structure of the church, then everything was arranged well according to him.

The Puritans could just have been able to live with that. They regarded James as the divine Prince who would very slowly push religion in the right direction. But already before sixteen twenty – as you can and could see in our Stratford – tensions in reference to religion just rose.

Under James' son Charles it is totally a different story. Though at first everyone thought highly of him, because of his stance against Spain, it now appears that he clearly has less charisma than his father. He doesn't have the talent of language, is taciturn and if he does speak he stumbles over his words. He is not able to bring parliament, the Privy Council and the court into line. The Puritans begin to distrust him. Their power is increasing and that of the middle and lower classes too. Thus the country-squires of the House of Commons want more control and the King increasingly despises them. He begins to see parliament as an obstacle to governing. He is very formal and does not tolerate contradiction. He is at odds with France, since both parties do not agree about the conditions under which his marriage is settled.

The Crown is increasingly in need of money, says John, and they who do not want a title, have to pay because they have declined the honor. Hall, for example, must pay ten pounds and William Combe fifteen. They prefer to do this rather than to admit and adjust.

Our son-in-law to be is a convinced supporter of the King. He also has a weak spot for the consort of the Majesty, Henrietta Maria. If she ever will visit Stratford with her revenue, he would open up his house at once for her, he says. We would not stop him there, but tease him with the costs that would entail.

Anyway, our Eliza would prefer to keep her wedding simple, but also so that as much as possible poor people can enjoy it. Our darling and her Thomas will have to grow towards one another, but who doesn't...

She looks up to her fiancé, also because he is nearly twice as old as she is. Our sweetheart is only just eighteen. She would also like me to take care of a few things, to tackle any mischief. Of course she requires the Bible in her room. In addition, she wants a twig of broom at her wedding bed with St. John's wort and a little flax on the floor. I have to put under the marital bed a sock, a pair of red ribbons and some bread and salt. She herself will set her shoes with the toes turned away from the bed. I will for the last time cooperate in this and I won't tell anyone. Everything to have my little one feel confident.

She is already quite a lady of course, but we both see in her still the little apple of our eye. The curly hair peeping unruly from under her tiny bonnet, dark blond and with golden lustre in the sun. Strenuously and care-free busy in the backyard. Her sweet wisps of hair moistly plastered down above her collar. The round toddler cheeks pinky red from observing the teeming critters in the earth. And then suddenly her big brown enquiring eyes upwards at you. If I lifted her up I smelled the sweet scent of the baby skin. When she wore her hair loose, she swept her locks short-tempered behind her ears, so that you saw the sunlight shine through her thin auricles. She picked with her tiny fists the most delicate summer bunches for John and me. And also for grandmother Hathaway, dear Anne, whom she loved so dearly and vice versa.

She is sad, Eliza, that Shakespeare and Anne cannot be here, at her wedding. Father's been dead for exactly ten years now, mother for nearly three and Thomas his father four already. Such is life, my sweet treasure. Fortunately the mother of Thomas, Mary Nash, can be present, at least if her health permits.

Meanwhile, Hall attends so many patients, among whom are still regularly the servants of the nobility. Recently he was at Alice Collins, who is companion and waiting-maid to lady Puckering of the

Warwick Priory. The father of Alice served previously as a lawyer for Shakespeare and drafted and witnessed the will of father. He was chosen in Stratford as successor of Thomas Greene, but unfortunately died a few months later.

Alice is twenty-four years old and she is tormented by the 'mother', hysterical attacks, and obstruction of her courses. After an attack she burst into tears. Her urine was thin as spring water. Hall had her well purged with a mixture of bryony roots. Of this every morning for a few days, she drank hot, five fluid ounces. After that she was quieter and healed well.

Luckily Hall was back in time for the wedding. She looked stunning, our Eliza. She is so wonderfully fresh and beaming and she walked so expectantly arm in arm with her Thomas. Her long shiny hair was elaborately brushed and hung nicely alongside her shoulders, while it still could. Behind her came the leading girls from the region, who are not yet married. Some carried a wedding cake, others garlands of fine gold plated wheat.

They are, like us, married from New Place and have covered the same way to our church, along the Churchway, under the trees to the Northern porch of Holy Trinity. It seems like yesterday that John and I walked there in our wedding procession, but that really is nearly nineteen years ago. Thomas Wilson has married them. My John cannot have wished better.

Later, in July, Hall had to travel in a hurry to Mary Beaumont, countess of Northampton, who, like the servant of father Nash, was tormented by jaundice, but in the seventh month of her pregnancy though. She is born from noble offspring and is obviously noticeably well brought up. Hall calls her very good in terms of disposition, 'very fair and beautiful'. In addition to the yellow discoloration the poor lady was experiencing some sort of tertian fever, severe pain in belly and head, and back problems. With her twenty-six years she asked Hall's advice, but refused to be purged.

Hall prescribed her a caudle, in which she decidedly wanted no rosewater. He was on the go for a few weeks with the noblewoman. Without using laxatives and emetics because of her pregnancy, Hall

knew how to treat her with yet other medicines. He told that the honorable lady was healed with herbs on her feet and a poultice on her back. She was brought to bed afterwards with a daughter, he said, whom he saw blooming with health in her arms.
We then still have had to bury brother-in-law Dive, John's brother, which we could barely handle, as it remained so busy with patients. It didn't stop. Day and night it went through. I think it will never be otherwise. Good intentions do not help.

The following year Hall has also treated Mary Nash, mother-in-law of Eliza. As slim as our Eliza still is, as bloated is Mary. Mistress Nash is now sixty-two and has long been troubled by consumption. Now she is also tormented by flatulence, and heat, making her sweat from navel to crown, especially after eating meat. Hall had had strained different ingredients through a Hippocras bag, which is a woolen bag, with which one filters out hearty wine with herbs. Each morning she had to take three drachm of it. An enema with linseed oil had a favorable result and with a syrup according to prescription after the art by the apothecary, she was not windy anymore. Then she was able to eat again. Mary said that she felt very well for a long time afterwards.

Also Eliza and Thomas, who now are married for a year, were happy for her. We hope that their marriage may be blessed with a child, or perhaps with several children, who knows. How will it be to become grandfather and grandmother of an own grandchild? I should not want to anticipate events and wait and pray humbly.

# XXVIII
# HALL CHURCHWARDEN AND SUSANNA ILL AGAIN

Near the end of the year sixteen twenty eight Hall nevertheless still became churchwarden for Wilson. He finds that he must support His Reverence, since the Corporation is getting annoyed at the man. Initially, the members of the Corporation backed up Wilson - they had his house neatly refurbished and gave him an increased wage. When he was temporarily excommunicated about four years ago by Bishop Thornborough, they stood up one and all for him. The following year, they assigned to him another twenty pounds, for his work in the parish during the previous plague epidemic.

The year was, however, not yet over but the mood had changed. Wilson had overplayed his hand anyhow. Apparently he had become overconfident and in their eyes too greedy. He had, after all the praises, appropriated too much timber from the churchyard. The Corporation had always been jealous of that right held by him. They threatened to withdraw those twenty pounds again and they have – how hurtful – invited Robert Harris of Hanwell to give the sermon each week.

Thus Hall decided to become churchwarden to help Wilson. I am concerned. If my Hall does something, he does it well, more than well. To be churchwarden is a lot of work. You have to closely monitor the churchgoers and their behavior. You have to act like a schoolmaster. You need to rebuke the blasphemers and those who put a hand under a woman's skirt, the drunkards and the latecomers. When the Sabbath is desecrated in some way, for example when one appears in church with one's hat on, or curses, or hangs around during the sermon outside the church, you must maintain authority. My Hall has much authority by nature, but do not ask how much time and extra energy this costs him.

What is more, he is watched closely when he - as a doctor - treats recusants, for example Mary Talbot of Grafton, Worcestershire. She comes from one of the wealthiest Catholic families, like the Fortescues and the Winter family of the gunpowder plot. Of course he also looks after these people. What does it matter how Catholic, Protestant or Puritan someone is?

Lady Talbot had acute scurvy with leaden spots on the thighs and corroded gums. Hall has helped her well. And at the beginning of March he treated Catholic Simon Underhill of Idlicote – also with scurvy. It has struck Hall that it occurs so often just after the winter months, this disease. We need to purge our body well in spring, and those of the children, to drive out the bad humors of winter.

My husband had to visit also Catholic Katherine Sturley, the corpulent daughter of the late Abraham Sturley, in our Stratford. She passed blood in her urine and that is not healthy. Hall has helped her extensively and healed her perfectly.

Slowly but surely it made bad blood with the Stratford church-goers, that he also attends to Catholic people. That was where the shoe pinched and Hall could not keep up the combination with his ordinary work. On the seventh of April sixteen twenty nine he resigned his position as a churchwarden.

That was a good thing too. Throughout the year it remained so busy with patients and the following spring I myself was tormented with scurvy. We write on the ninth of February sixteen thirty and my Hall has written a comprehensive report on it.

He noted it approximately like this, if I remember correctly: 'Wife was troubled with the Scurvy, accompanied with Pain of the Loins, Corruption of the Gums, stinking Breath, Melancholy, Wind, Cardiac Passion, Laziness, difficulty in breathing, fear of the Mother, binding of the Belly and torment there, and all of a long continuance, with restlessness and weakness.' By Cardiac Passion he means a fainting fit, so I don't remember.

I, who am as clean as a new pin as far as my body goes, and always want to make a good impression, so ill and miserable. I didn't dare to breathe, I thought it was very awful for John and was embarrassed. And then this wretched flatulence. Let it go anyhow, Hall said, everything can come out but better. But I did not want this. I did not want to be like this in front of my husband. I can imagine the desperation of seriously ill clients at such a moment even more clearly. Let alone of those who die...

Hall gave me an electuary of tamarind and cremortart. On my back he put a poultice with saffron, pitch, resin and myrrh. Next day, the tenth, I thought I was all right again. Recklessly I managed to catch a cold and everything got worse. I had a terrible pain in my joints and couldn't even lie in my bed. When they tried to help me turn over, I cried out.

Hall anointed me and put the poultice on again. That softened beneficially. I was so grateful and relieved, that I could laugh a bit and had a nice night. Again and again I fell asleep and so got some rest. If I just woke up for a while in between, I enjoyed it that I saw my doctor next to me in bed.

But in the morning I got abdominal pain and severe wind anew. Hall got out of bed quickly and still in his night attire, he made me a sweetened purge to an old recipe of one Sennert. To this had to be added wine, prepared with steel, according to Crato, which always has to be drawn eight days au Bain-Marie on a fire. That John luckily had made already. When I was healed again, I asked our servants to replace all the bedding and to wash and bleach the nightgowns. Our bedroom they have aired, refreshed and supplied with fresh flowers and herbs.

That same year sixteen thirty Hall also visited Spencer Compton, Lord Northampton, who was twenty-nine years old. It is an honor to be able to treat the nobleman. Our dear Queen Elizabeth was his godmother and when Compton married Mary Beaumont nine years ago, King James has been his honored guest. He has also always been very much in favor with Prince Charles who, once he was King, appointed him as his Chamberlain.

The noble patient was suffering from a terrible quinsy. He could barely breathe and he drooled a sticky fluid. Normally Hall would have bled him from under the tongue. In such a case, that is the best cure, but the highborn man decidedly did not want to have this.

Then Hall proceeded to a gargle, a hot poultice and a very strong purge. That worked well, but for a short time.

My Hall got slightly piqued when they still let doctor Clayton of Oxford come that night. Clayton recommended the same bloodletting my John had wanted to apply, which the ill Compton kept refusing. The Oxford doctor prescribed cough lozenges then and also a poultice. Hall described extensively for me which ingredients the latter contained: the dirt of two swallow's nests with straw, and the feces of a white dog. This while my Hall had used in his poultice purely green wormwood and hogs grease. He had to admit, however, that the patient was redeemed from pain and danger.

Then he could save face again by giving lady Northampton a prescription of his against her own quinsy. Also he was allowed to give the nobleman among other things a further gargle against the swelling of his throat. Thus the two doctors solved it anyway with combined efforts and the couple was cured.

Cured, oh divine word. Shall the distinguished gentleman have been just as relieved as I was, when I felt healed again and refreshed. Thank you God, thank you Hall. I would never spread such a smell anymore. Forgive me, John. How well I will take care of myself and you both. I will be strong. That you won't need to think, my dear, of melancholy again or even worse of hysteria. I blush anew as I think back on myself in that state. Yet I know far too well that some things happen to a human being. You cannot control everything yourself where illness and health are concerned.

As for vicar Wilson, the Corporation allowed again to the reverend man at the end of this year the extra twenty pounds. This, provided he tolerates Robert Harris of Hanwell for another year beside him as curate. But something inside of me tells me this won't help for long...

# XXIX
# GREAT PRESSURE ON HALL

Everyone is asking Hall for advice. You name it, he has treated it. It ranges from miscarriages and infertility to worms, dropsy and the dreaded plague.

He visited three times over the past few months thirteen year young Mary Combe, eldest daughter of the annoying William Combe. The little lady had female obstructions, symptoms of hysteria, convulsions about the eyes and headaches. Of course Hall treats her as best he can, including a pill that is covered with a fine layer of gold leaf. The fault lies not with the noble girl that she has such a father. The treatment of all people equally and proportionately is what matters.

In addition, Hall is trying to keep up with his professional literature as well as possible. Thus he is engrossed lately in the new discoveries of doctor William Harvey. The very knowledgeable doctor and anatomist graduated in Cambridge at Caius College and works in London. He has discovered that the blood is being pumped through the heart by the veins and has published this in his book 'De Motu Cordis et Sanguinis'. It seems to be that the heart is continually contracting and circulates the blood thus through the body. From the right so-called ventricle, the blood then goes through the lung and from there to the left ventricle of the heart, and thus all the time. No wonder that the very learned Harvey is also a doctor at the court of King Charles. It is extremely interesting. It should be obligatory as a doctor to keep up with each new development.

For Hall his work comes always first and foremost. My father could cope with a lot of things at once, but my Hall cannot combine everything. I think that's understandable, because his practice is about life and death. If you are a doctor in Stratford and the surrounding area, people ask your help and advice daily regarding their constitution, but also on secondary matters. They want, for example, that he puts in a word for them at the Corporation or at the church, that he supports and comforts in loss or difficulties, that he mediates in conflicts in families and in matters of business. When the doctor is not at home, then people come to me for advice or by way of me to Hall anyway.

In all this he still wastes his energy to the church. And also the Corporation always appeals urgently to him. Hall didn't want to, but in May of this year – we are writing already in sixteen thirty-two – they have elected him 'chief-burgess' of the city. Previously he had on two occasions managed to wriggle out of it and to apologize neatly. But now they make him bend, while they know he can hardly handle everything at once. Maybe they pushed through to get hold of him because of his support to Wilson.

But there you are - he had to cry off immediately. He was marked down as an absentee on the attendance register of June the thirtieth. It reads: *'Jo[hannes] Hall, generosus, in Artibus Magister, a[bsens],'* and added is the notation that: 'Master Hall, at the last hall elected a chief-burgess of this Borough, hath neglected to come to take his oath, being thereunto warned by both the Chamberlains and Serjeants.'

For the date of the sixth of July he got again a warning, but it was because of an important and compelling gentleman that he had to excuse himself.

He often has to deal with changing moods and bad tempers of people. Now take such a letter from that gent, Sidney Davenport. Here it is. It is dated the fifth of July of this year and reads as follows:

'Good Mr Hall

*I sent my boy to you this morning to carrie my water & acquaint you with what daunger & extremitie I am faullen into in respect my shortness of breath & obstructions of my liver, that I cannot sleep nor take anie rest, and although I have more need of yr presence this daie than to stay untill to morrow yet in regard of the multitude of yr affairs being ye Markett daie yet I well hoped you would not have failed me to morrow morning being fridaie at 7 of the clock in the morning, for I will not eat or drink untill I see you.'*

Thus the letter continues, almost without full stops or commas. If the man speaks just as he writes, I can imagine that the good soul suffers from shortness of breath:

*'My owne Servante is not yet returned from Stratford, but about dynner time this daie I received a note from you howe that you cannot be here at Bushwood with me to morrow in respect of some private meeting at yr hall concerning the affairs of yr Towne you saie you are warned to be there & if you be absent you are threatened to be fined,'*

In other words, the gentleman doesn't believe my Hall, and he thinks there is another sick person involved, instead of business of the borough. And also that he does not want to assume that John can be fined for his absence, since a doctor is pre-eminently needed with his patients, and should be busy with his studies of diseases.

Master Sidrak Davenport concludes with best wishes and cordial greetings and hopes that God will protect him (Hall) and that he always remains: *'Yor trewly loving friend & Servant'*.

But then again though, better than expected. I myself have thought of somewhat more punctuation marks for this letter, because he goes on rattling at a stretch. You can see well how forceful the man is. He pleads for himself, and is insistent upon and suspicious about Hall and he is not the only one doing so. In the beginning of our marriage I would have certainly taken this very much to heart. I would have been concerned about the patients and the reputation of Hall. I would have worried and I sure would have lain awake to think that someone lost his temper like that with my John.

It leaves me still not quite untouched, but over the years I have learned, that this goes with the job, and that people have a right to their reproaches, which arise mostly out of panic. Hall should never take it personally, and I certainly not. He has also taught me to distinguish between what is personal and what is business, and to be always flawless in my words and always do my best. I should note how miserable people can feel.

And yet I can see by the looks of John, for example, by a grim and determined expression about his mouth, when he is annoyed. And at first I am still indignant at such an insolent letter. But at the same moment when John then asks me what I think of it, he immediately calms down. Then he is again professional, he can leave the problem with the other person, whom he calls choleric, but whom he also takes seriously. I don't remember if he went to Davenport, but I assume he will have done so. In any case, he missed the council meeting that day.

In the end my Hall was not sworn in until July the eleventh, nota bene while even though it should be noted that they had called him 'a hornet in a hornet's nest'. If he would have taken a strong line, he would have withdrawn immediately...

I hold my breath... I'm sure it is too much for him. He himself knows it like no other, but when they ask you so often and so emphatically, and you are not clear-headed anymore because your head is reeling, you say: Yes...

Soon after, a very serious, highly contagious epidemic broke loose. How many times that has occurred. And all those times my dear himself has survived. A man is getting older, much more vulnerable and more susceptible. We can only pray...

# XXX
# DOCTOR HALL HIMSELF ILL

We write in August sixteen thirty-two. He has not said to me at all that he has been walking with violently bleeding hemorrhoids, what is more while he had to make so many visits in the area. And on horseback too.

On August the thirteenth he left for Susanna Vernon in Hanbury, Worcestershire, wife of the vicar there. The poor woman - John calls her 'religious, well-formed and beautiful' - had the many symptoms of scurvy and also coldness of the feet. Hall has treated her with all possible means and also with bryony water against hysterical attacks. The successful treatment took many days, after which he rode back again, still with those hemorrhoids!

Once he got home he really had to roll up his sleeves. The bubonic plague was attacking the village and killing almost every ill person, within just a few days. Unfortunately, it is the most common form of the plague and it is a horrible affection. The whole body is covered with the evil lumps that can discharge pus and burst. Large painful gland swellings may occur, among other things in the groins. It goes hand in hand with high fever, and may later turn into pneumonia.

My fear regards my Eliza and of course my John, my concern goes for the whole of Stratford. Hall has worked to do what he could. He has not allowed himself any rest. Day and night he was ready to help the people, including in the neighborhood. Sometimes he had the horses harnessed to ride again even in the middle of the night. Then I watched him, how he disappeared in the dark, with his waving doctor's mantle streaming behind, with his medicine case at the back. I tried to put it out of my mind that he himself could be affected, but now my fears have come true. It was bound to come: the doctor himself is ill!

First he was crazy with the pain in his teeth and he was felled by the burning fever, which nearly killed all who were infected. To see your husband suffer like that, makes a human being feel so powerless and desperate. I have begged and prayed: let him live, Lord. Stay with me, do not leave me, John.

It was terrible to see… the convulsions of mouth and eyes. Initially, he still made an attempt to treat himself with a rigorous purgative of rhubarb but, aside from four stools, that did almost nothing to help. Then John used the decoction of hartshorn and you would say that the disease then came out through the urine, because it flowed for four days. This gave us a little bit of hope, but John was getting skinnier and was so weakened that he himself could no longer turn over in bed without assistance. Also I helped all I could until it became too heavy for my back.

By now he had lost control of all his limbs and was delirious. He indicated with his last strength, to cut open a dove alive and put it on his feet, to draw the bad vapors out of them. Never have I seen and heard that from the poor beast, but now: everything, everything to cure my love.

Then he was delirious again, my dear, my spouse, my John, my all. I prayed my most fervent prayers and kept up Halls motto: 'Health is from the Lord'. We applied another enema with soothing herbs, a bleeding from the liver vein and leeches on the hemorrhoids, but at my wits' end I had two of his friends and colleagues called, including master Bowles.

His colleagues prescribed him an electuary with all kinds of anti-scorbutic means, containing bugloss and violets, wood sorrel syrup, lemon and oil of vitriol. Later, he was purged with senna and cassia, mixed with absinthe water. In addition, he had at bedtime an opiate of a mixture with red poppy heads, an ointment for the back and a poultice in the heart region. They also carried out bloodletting again and applied leeches to the hemorrhoids, and once more anew decoctions of hartshorn, making him quite able to eat a bit.

Then, in turn, John could take over himself and took a little strengthening 'chalibiat' wine, wine with prepared steel. Against the pain in the teeth he used, I believe, laurel oil. Suddenly he was troubled with itch in his scrotum – that was all he needed - which was healed with our decoction of sarsaparilla with anti-scorbutic herbs.

All in all, it took no less than five weeks, from August the twenty-seventh to September the twenty-ninth, but God be thanked and praised, my darling 'became perfectly well'!

While the poor Sidrak Davenport though died a month later, three months after he had written that letter to Hall. Would the noble gentleman have already felt then his impending death?

My John himself began with this prayer in his notes about his own illness:

*'Thou, oh Lord, which hast the power of Life and Death, and drawest from the Gates of Death, I confess, without any Art or Counsel of Man, but only from thy Goodness and Clemency, thou hast saved me from the bitter and deadly Symptoms of a deadly Fever, beyond the expectation of all about me, restoring me as it were from the very jaws of Death to former health; for which I praise thy Name, O most merciful God, and Father of our Lord Jesus Christ, praying thee to give me a most thankful Heart for this great favour, for which I have cause to admire thee.'*

I think our love is getting deeper and deeper over the years. How can that be so? Shall we never see the last of it? Sometimes I thought: do we not exaggerate? Don't we make it more beautiful than it is? But I have experienced it like this again, when I almost had to lose him...

I would want to overwhelm him with a thousand kisses, my John. I would like to hold him in my arms for days on end, and only set him free when we have to eat.

Our existence is one big exercise in getting to know ourselves better, and then taking the other as he or she is. That is probably the hardest and that takes a lifetime. And every once in a while you come a step closer to your own darkness. You assume initially that you don't own darkness to a large extent. But if you look more closely at yourself, you can shed more light on the other person. Then you see his or her beautiful traits of character earlier. And then you can also forgive the traits that might be somewhat less favorable. And in the long run, you will estimate them as not being so very bad or on the contrary pretty good. The latter because you understand that you were the one who judged incorrectly all this time and too quickly. That really is a lifelong process, but if it succeeds, great love and passion can enhance a whole life.

Look at me now, I could stand on the pulpit for the whole community like this, and then I would shout: my Hall, my John, my dearest is cured again, people! Thanked be the Lord!
Once one knows that the doctor is recovered, the stream of patients gets going again, with in addition to the terrible epidemic the other ailments too. Here in Old Stratford he visited Katherine, wife of the troublesome William Combe. Hall has treated her with no rancour in the circumstances with drastic means for a long-standing serious scurvy. Couldn't that Combe have watched her better? The poor woman fortunately was freed by Hall of her symptoms and gave birth shortly thereafter, beyond all expectations, to a goodly daughter. On the fourth of October little Constance was baptized.

Then he rode all the way to Frances Fiennes of Broughton Castle, Oxfordshire. After the birth of her second child the midwife had given her juice of lemons and wood sorrel. Thereupon patient had fallen into a hydropic swelling of the right thigh and the right leg. The midwife had applied to this a poultice with red lead. Hall diagnosed the case scorbutic dropsy and gave her a lick on a licorice stick to reduce the amount of phlegm in the lungs. Then he prescribed ten recipes, four before he was called away for all kinds of other pressing issues, and six after he had come back. The patient had an enema twice a week with child's urine, in which leaven was cooked.

Baby Constance Combe couldn't last out until Christmas. Eight days after her birth her sad parents had to let her go again. It always is a bitter blow when a little one cannot survive. When I see the shaken parents bury the innocent child I feel it all the way through to my marrow and bone. You can still dislike someone, but at the same time you wouldn't wish that on your worst enemy. It often happens and one never will get used to it.

They say the Lord has a purpose in everything. It may then seem hard in this regard, but we should be all the more grateful that we and Stratford have been able to retain doctor Hall!

# XXXI
# PEWS AND LADIES

Hall's practice and work remain under pressure. Today he treated the eighty six year old John Thornborough, Bishop of Worcester. A special man. He is very learned in religion, chemistry, politics and science. But he's also said to be fond of hunting, fencing, dancing and flirting with the girls.

He is relentless towards recusants. He strongly renounces the 'superstitions of Rome', as he calls it. He does not have a very good reputation with his divorces, against the will of the Majesty. His eldest son committed suicide at the age of twenty, related to gambling debts, as is rumored. It all seems a bit messy.

The man had some kind of gout, not real gout, as his own doctor suggested. His urine was changeable and he had 'livid spots' in his thighs. Salt humors and vapors ascended to his head, giving him restless nights. If he slept well, then he was very anxious. The cause of this might be the sudden murder of a family member, after which Bishop John became very melancholic. Sometimes he had pain in one foot and then again in his knee, with swellings around the knee and the instep.

Hall told him he could be relieved but not entirely cured. The man was already well purged and too weak to undergo that again. He was given a gel of hartshorn, partridge and also knuckles of veal, with raisins, dates and anti-scorbutic herbs. Live worms were put on the swellings. The feet were bathed in ten handfuls of brooklime, well boiled in a sufficient amount of beer for a bath, morning and evening. After the bath he got a hot poultice of wormwood powder with egg yolks. The Reverend had no more pain and he could go out again. Ladies, beware!

The Bishop was satisfied and it seemed to Hall a good moment to ask him and master Wilson for another pew. I myself did not think it was really necessary. We are sitting close to the beautiful pulpit, traditionally the pew for the Shakespeares, on the south side of the nave of the church. I'm attached to it. But Hall has set his heart on the extreme north side of the nave, where the senior aldermen and their wives take their permanent seats within living memory.

The Bailiff and his aldermen are angry of course, especially since Hall had lodged a complaint against them for breach of contract with Wilson. Then there was the devil to pay, and huge friction between both parties. It ran so high that the Vicar-General of the Archbishop of Canterbury had to set up an investigation.

Before, Hall actually couldn't do anything wrong lately. He and our Thomas Nash had paid a lot to repair the church and we had also donated the expensive pulpit with the sophisticated carvings. So the recently cured Bishop had drafted the following act under his episcopal seal. I quote:

*'That the said Master Hall and his wife, and Master Nash and his wife, and Mistress Woodward and Mistress Lane, should have the seat now in question, to and for them to sit and kneel in if the same seat were large enough for them.'*

But why take things easy, when you can make a fuss? Mutually the accusations were still hotting up between, on the one hand, the church, Hall and Wilson, and on the other hand the Corporation. I didn't quite recognize my own John, but I understood him though. He had just sold our own tithes at a hundred pounds less, hoping that Wilson might get another sixty and the schoolmaster twenty. And while certainly the gentlemen members of the Corporation did not remain polite and decent anymore, Hall was short tempered and abusive.

So much so, that he - I remember it well - early in January sixteen thirty three, to be precise on the eleventh, was called for because of his offensive language towards the authorities. They said that my John was 'acrimonious and quarrelsome' and they have also stated that on the Minutes of the meeting.

The church was not having this and denounced them to the Supreme Court of the Chancery with the same complaints that Hall had expressed. The Corporation members found that allegation in their turn scandalous and returned accusations against Wilson. And so it went on and I really would have liked my John not to have interfered.

In the meantime, it seems to become more crowded in the practice this year. He is giving treatment to many ladies. If everyone would come to our home, then it would go all right maybe but the riding and travelling time begin to take their toll. He himself will never complain of it, my darling, but he also is already way past fifty and I can tell by his face when he actually can no longer take much more.

For example, he rides to the noble countess of Northampton and further on to the granddaughter of Sir Edward Greville in Warwick Castle. Then at once to lady Rainsford, for whom Hall has great respect.

He did have to visit Lady Rainsford at Clifford Chambers, which is fortunately just outside Stratford. She is now sixty-two years of age and still equally beautiful, it seems, despite her grief over the loss of her poet and admirer Michael Drayton, in December two years ago. The great poet and friend of father has been honorably buried in London, at Westminster Abbey.

The night before he died, Drayton has written yet another poem for her, his muse….. that he loved her so much, that he would rather die than ever having to live a day without her. He spent two or three months every summer with the Rainsford couple at Clifford Chambers on their estate. In sixty-four sonnets Drayton has always sung about his love for the lady. You just have to condone that as a husband, even though the poet was a meek man.

In his work 'Polyolbion' he glorified their place and also our Warwickshire. In it he notes the medicinal plants of the area and praises a pious learned physician. Will he perhaps have meant my Hall by that? Hall has treated him, when he suffered from a tertian fever. A mixture with a violet syrup worked wonders, both upwards and downwards.

As for her own husband, Sir Henry, it is more than ten years since he died. The lady still opens her house to literate people and their conversation in the French language. Hall describes her as 'modest, pious, friendly' and so on. For a long time I have been able to take it very well; as well as the enemas he has had to give her…

Here in Stratford it is also still always busy of course. So it happened that the poor wife of vicar Wilson had hysterical attacks again because of all the commotion around her husband. Anne Wilson had travelled to Bath for hydrotherapy, to doctor Lapworth. But she drunk way too much of the St. Vincent's well, because she thought that she could get rid of a stone in this way, of which Hall doubted the existence. On her journey home, in very bad weather, she suffered attacks with fainting and paralyses.

Hall was, when he arrived home, called in at once. He gave her a purge bole with bryony against the hysteria, a remedy for flatulence and an enema. Against fainting my Hall gave a powder, which he always carries with him. That is a kind of volatile salt, made of thirty-one ingredients, including pearl, red coral and musk. He will never leave without this panacea in his medicine chest. Also this time it worked fast and excellently. Mistress Wilson was delivered from all complaints and danger of death.

So many patients, but that's not what keeps him awake at night. Those are usually the things around them. Those are the annoyances around borough decisions, political misrule and alleged injustice. These are matters such as those around Wilson and the pew question. Fortunately, people now realize - we write in October sixteen thirty-three - that doctor Hall cannot cope with extra obligations to the city council. It was about time.

# XXXII
# MORE MELANCHOLY

It is already March sixteen thirty-five. Two years ago we took over the lease for Judith of her home 'the Cage', which her husband Thomas Quiney could not pay anymore. We had to help her for the benefit of herself and her sons. We do this together with our Thomas Nash and vicar in Harbury, Richard Watts, the other brother-in-law of Thomas Quiney. The situation had got out of control. Quiney could no longer maintain his family.

Those taverns... we already have so many vintners being ruined by their own trade and our brother-in-law is no different. I pity him as much as anything. He has many qualities though. He is so proficient in French and philosophizes nicely in that language. His motto is: 'Blessed is the man who learns wisdom from other's follies', and that in French...

The whole thing was hurtful for them, but there was no other solution. Thomas had been fined several times already and could no longer meet his obligations. His Judith could with our help in any case continue to live in the Cage. She has mustered up all her energy and has the property converted into a private house.

She makes the best of it. She had imagined things differently, when they married. Then she looks at us and then just stays so quiet. And then I look at her, who had to lose her first son... Sorrow can make a human being so melancholic.

How many kinds of melancholy are there? The musical Leonard Kempson had suffered from it and now take for example master John Trapp, who was treated today by Hall. We write on the eleventh of March. The good man succeeded Alexander Aspinall as schoolmaster of the Grammar School and he is the curate in Trinity Church. My John has just made notes about him in the evening in his observations:

> 'Mr. John Trap, (Minister, for his piety and learning second to none) about the 33 year of his age, of a melancholy temper, and by much Study fell into Hypochondriac Melancholy, and pain of the Spleen, with some Scorbutic Symptoms, viz. difficulty of breathing after gentle motion of the Body, beating of the Heart, with fainting at the rising of the Vapours, and became a little better when they were dispersed.'

For days on end medication was alternated, that I do know. Pulp of apples and cremortart and steeled wine came into it. That cremortart, I am told, is 'cremor tartari', which is Latin for 'mush from hell'. It's a good thing the clergyman does not know that... There was purging and drinking wine, after which the reverend man was quite a bit more cheerful. Then again cream of tartar. And anti-scorbutic beer. All in all the treatment lasted for weeks, in which he also took the medicine 'Manus Christi', beneficial as a counterpart of that mush from hell. Manus Christi, that's a medicine with sugared damask roses onto marble. Then the curate wanted again the medicines with wine and beer, of which he said that these gave him the best hope of recovery. And so he was with God's blessings saved from the jaws of death and healed well, for which he heartily thanked my Hall.

Dear Master Trapp. Constantly with his nose in his books, and thereby melancholic. That is true. He always seems so cast down and absorbed in thought. That is his nature. And that's why he reads a lot and lives through reading. Or is it the other way around? It will match anyway, I think. Not everyone can be equally exuberant. Melancholy, the words say it all: 'melas chole' is Greek for black bile, through which you have a dark complexion and a meditative disposition. We all however have a little bit of that in us, and sometimes - for example when we are in mourning - threefold. But there are people who always have it, and there are those who always have it very much. I don't know what's worse, Hall says then, the suffering of the body or the deep suffering of the spirit. Both are torment. Maybe that of the mind is one's disposition in the first instance already, as with the silent people and the readers. They can think themselves all the way down, without any reason. They are hard on themselves and just keep thinking that they are insignificant and good-for-nothing. That you see also with people who have a lot of talent. And also with very busy people, who cover up their gloominess, contrary to themselves.

By now, I have an eye for it, both through experience in life and in practice. I can see it in the eyes of these people. How busy one sometimes seems and joins in with the others, and yet the eyes do not participate. Often the mouth is also somewhat tighter. Most people are unaware that someone is like that and that helps such a person then again to behave just as normally as possible. I would like to embrace them and take them in my arms, but it would be weird to do that all of a sudden and people will talk again. It would also help only for a while. Melancholy continues to agonize if one suffers from life. Nothing will be good enough and everything meaningless. They say: keep praying, and that helps a little bit, but then again they feel so trapped. Maybe they would do better to go outside. With people who work on the land it occurs much less, says Hall. But even then you see it though. Melancholia - I will never downplay the issue. How complex a human being is.

Then the melancholy of Edith Stoughton from St. John's, Warwick, is yet different. She was at the age of seventeen miserably tormented by it. Until then her monthly bleedings had not yet broken through. She had hysterical attacks. Hall told how she got angry at her close friends very quickly, as she always screamed that her parents would kill her, just like all the others who approached her. Imagine.

She had been well purged by skilled doctors, but still her father wanted her to be examined by Hall to see whether a cure would be possible. To which Hall had replied that it would be very difficult, since she had a melancholic constitution, which was dominated by the black bile, with severe symptoms of agony and delusions.

Hall prescribed two days of enemas with tartar. That works well against this dark melancholy, which is hot and dry. The one of master Trapp is cold and dry. When she was somewhat quieter, he carried out, among other things, bloodletting on her left arm. Next day he advised her father after the purging, that she had to be let alone as much as possible.

Later, when she was more approachable, Hall prescribed some medications and a diacodium, poppy syrup, to let her sleep and sweat. And so, by the blessing of God, she was freed from her attacks. The preponderance of my spouse will also have helped.

When I see him toil like that, my John, I think sometimes that I detect in his features a tinge of melancholy too. With his compulsion to exercise his profession of course as effectively as possible, he can be so strict with himself. If things don't come off the way he wants, and he feels thwarted by the Corporation, he can even be choleric. When he then also maybe has had to abandon one of his patients to death, it is too much for a human being.

Then I have to take good care of him at home. When he has spent so much energy, placed all his hope in it, to keep someone alive, and it turns out badly, then he must come to terms with it. Especially with children and at the time, with the young George Quiney, for example, he was overcome by grief. It happens regularly, of course, it is part of the job, but each time he is set back too. At home he is in that case quieter than otherwise. I know right away that something is wrong. I wait as patiently as possible until he comes out with his story. And when it comes to that, he will tell it all in detail. I learned to listen and I won't intertwine my own story then.

I always have to put up with it myself too. When a human life is lost, it also makes me repeatedly sad. And yet I feel at the same time usually a counterforce in me. Something inside of me forces me to think about more cheerful things then. For example, the comedies of father, and his masquerades, Puck in his Midsummer Night's Dream or the cheerful audience in the Globe. And without mentioning these plays and with a lot of respect for the relatives, it seems I always find somewhere something to catch hold of to cheer them and Hall up a little.

# XXXIII
# HALL'S WORRIES AND THE PLAGUE ONCE AGAIN

We write in autumn sixteen hundred thirty-five. The cows and sheep will once again be slaughtered, salted, smoked and dried, to get us through the winter. So the seasons are stringing together. Sometimes I realize with a shock, that sweet master Shakespeare was my age now, fifty-two, when he died. With the passage of years comes the realization that the birth dates of the patients are moving up too compared to your own date. Before they were almost all older than I am, ever more frequently they are now the same age or younger.

Now take baronet Thomas Puckering of the Warwick Priory. I look not so much up to him, rather I look at him with respect. I think at first that he is older than I am, it turns out that he is only forty-four, eight years younger. The noble gentleman had terrible headaches. After treatment and with the help of God the patient was freed from all his symptoms, Hall said. He had a vein in his left arm as a preventive measure opened to remove his sharp humors. This took place mid-September.

Everyone wants my Hall to be their doctor. Then one lady writes to another that she is so happy that she has chosen Hall too, because she knows from personal experience how skilled he is. That she will put in a good word with the doctor, that he will come soon. So I hear during our entire marriage new stories by him about all kinds of people and their ailments. And while I have always worried whether it is not too much work and responsibility at the same time for my dear, the cases of the clients repeatedly intrigue him and me. You can compare it with your own life. Then you know how lucky you are yourself, and that we should not grieve for example that we have but one child. Though I do pray that our Eliza will become a mother one day.

But the main thing is that we should be grateful for our family. If it is convenient we have lunch together or sometimes even with Eliza, in the large kitchen. Those are such intimate moments. Most familiar is it when Hall comes between times in the kitchen for a while. Usually for some juice or a bowl of boiled water, for himself or for a nervous patient. I always set that out. When John is relaxed, I get a wink and then I know enough or if he puts his hand on my shoulder when I'm busy cooking. And very occasionally a fleeting kiss in my neck, if he is in a very happy mood.

After moving into New Place he got more and more work and there was less time for such moments. The issue with Wilson had not been of help. Also my John experienced friction again last year with the Corporation. Everything seemed settled concerning the pews, but we had to give our pews back again though to the wives of the burgesses. But Hall did have our pew assigned by the bishop himself. We had sat there for quite some time now and suddenly we had to choose which seat we wanted to keep and which to give up. Hall could no longer control himself. He would before have settled the matter amicably, but now he was seething with rage. He saw that the Corporation was stubborn as could be and thus, loyal as he is, he supported Wilson so much the more. Then they together again submitted a request to the Chancery for a salary increase for the vicar and, of course, of the schoolmaster too. Moreover, the Corporation still puts part of the money in its own pocket for private use and events, Hall said.

The Corporation has called in lawyers and last May Wilson had to return the key of the Chapel. In this way the stricken reverend could not even enter his own house. One claimed that he had desecrated the chancel of the church with superstition and had his children play there with balls, and that some dents had been made in the walls and panes were broken. That he had allowed pigs to lie and chickens to roost in the Guild Chapel and that laundry was hung to dry there. Well I do know that Wilson is not so very particular, but this was greatly exaggerated. Please excuse me, but they just are looking for excuses.

On the twelfth day of May the whole thing exploded. Mistress Ann Smith was buried. Hall had treated her last year in connection with a serious eye inflammation. Wilson had not been invited and was sitting on purpose on the steps of the pulpit, so curate Simon Trapp couldn't pass. On the fifth of June, on our wedding day, the diocese was called in again for investigation.

On the north side, to the extreme end of the nave of the church, we had that new pew assigned to us again and had to accept it within a month.

Fine, but what my John had not been able to swallow is that Wilson was then under pressure and so pleaded guilty to all the allegations against him. Then they had the venerable man on the sixteenth of July promptly suspended as punishment. This remained so only three months, because they knew very well how learned he was and that the parish could not do without his flamboyant speeches. The issue had all the while disturbed our Stratford. Almost everyone had been called to witness, from both sides. My John had nothing more to say.

And now, with a new epidemic of plague, I see only concern on the face of my dear. He has quickly become so grey and his complexion whitish. It is just as if he has shrunk and is walking somewhat crooked. Is it to be wondered? He feels so responsible. How much can a human being endure. The disease attacks with wolf's claws. One after another has to die a painful death. It is just as if a ghost haunts the streets. The ghost of the exasperating fear. The sick who are still alive have the most unsightly swellings and sores. Where these have burst, nasty pus is coming out. I must not think about that too much, otherwise I cannot eat anymore and I have to remain strong, though I'm afraid. Dear acquaintances and neighbors lose their loved ones and then it is their turn.

I do what I can, I help where I can. I listen, I dress wounds, I ask for patience, I explain, I see to cooling or a drink, I take the urine vials and the stories that go with it, and try to comfort wherever necessary. I want to assist Hall as much as possible and in the meantime keep my eye on my own health, that of Eliza and especially that of him. As far as he allows, for he will not give himself time to anything else but the patients. The people need him. They clamor or lisp with their last efforts for help. Or they are silent in their misery.

How sick a human being can feel. I pray and I pray and I'm trying to relieve the distress of anyone who knocks at the door. But what can I really do, except comfort, take care and comfort again. Every little bit helps, but I cannot save them. That I can leave only to the Lord. Hang on, Susanna, go on, Susanna. Keep on your feet and help your dear doctor. Hold on, Hall. Do what you can for the people. Do all in your power. Apply everything you have learned. But, please, please, please, stay alive, my sweet darling.

# XXXIV
# HALL DECEASED

My John is no more. He was so sick. Just like three years ago. But this time I felt that things would turn out differently. I have often felt with our townsfolk whether they would survive or not. Two of our neighbors were gone just before my love this week.

The plague haunts us everywhere in England. Tens of thousands have already died. Alone in the town of Hull there are three thousand dead, I've heard. My Hall has done what he could in our sweet Stratford and beyond. He seemed indefatigable. He has visited everyone and many people came to our door. They brought along with them the water from their masters or loved ones. The apothecaries have worked like madmen and Hall himself hardly slept.

A minute ago still patients knocked at the door. I told them the doctor is no longer among us. You saw it coming upon them with a shock. The doctor dead. They murmured condolences, or turned round without saying anything - on the verge of despair. They didn't dare to ask anything anymore, also with piety, I saw. They felt my own panic and disbelief. Formerly they still always asked for something, asked me in an extremely friendly way whether I perhaps could obtain a bit of laudanum. If the doctor was not in, then maybe his wife could alleviate or comfort, but now one understood... Something like this is spreading like wildfire through town.

And then it fell silent. As silent as it's never been here before. Before you could always expect someone with a request for help, but now there is silence even in the walls of our house.

It is already December. Snow covers the graves and the roofs, the banks of the Avon and the gardens. And our herb garden. Please bloom no more. Just don't come into bud in spring, plants. It isn't needed anymore. The doctor is dead. And the apothecaries will find work somewhere else.

However hard it might have been for Hall when it was freezing - on foot and on horseback - we still enjoyed together with our Eliza the winter fairyland outside. And then in the kitchen the warmth of the fireplace and the conviviality. And now, in this white world I hold only our inconsolable child in my arms. I myself am completely rudderless.

I sniff up your body odor out of your doctor's cloak. I fill your clothes with your loved form in my mind. At night I keep your nightclothes close to me - the only way to fall asleep. Then I hope fervently that you may appear in my dream. Your voice is in my ears, your breath in my body, your hands in my hands, your footstep in my heart, your thinking in my being. Never do I walk without you, your spirit in my soul, your love in my days. What is it that hurts so much? My arms that want to embrace and are just flailing in the air in silence, deafening silence and bitter loss. The loss that I will never be able to talk to you for a while again.

On your heavy tombstone in the parish church, next to the one of father, is our family coat of arms and an inscription in Latin, that says:

*'Hall is laid here, very renowned for his medical skill,*
*looking for the joys of the Kingdom of God.*
*Worthy was he, for his merits, to outdo Nestor in years,*
*but on earth a like Day lays hands on all.'*

'Very renowned for his medical skill': 'Medica celeberrimus arte', in Latin. My skillful, clever husband surely was renowned.

I myself could write no epitaph. A storm of feelings has prevented me from thinking. I feel as if my head would burst. Everything I would have wanted to put into words for you in a wonderful way, my love, but that's not how things work.

As I sit here, I get completely petrified. I gaze at your grave and hear or see nothing else. My eyes don't read and in my ears is only a murmuring sound. As if the Avon flows through my head. And tears won't come. Numb. Oh, darling. How cold feels death and how familiar. Soothing and frightening. My better half is no longer here. Eliza has no daddy anymore.

How do you comfort your child? You rock her in your arms. Already a woman of twenty-seven, but always our daughter, his girlie, his little one. All her grief comes out with her. She feels like crying all the time. This is also because she can never give Hall a grandchild anymore in his lifetime. He made her take spices still, hoping that... And that he, if she happens to get pregnant, will never see her child. I rock her and I rock her and I rock to comfort my own trembling lonely body too. I have asked her whether she wants to come and live here in New Place. Enough room there is with ten chambers and more. She thinks it over and will consult with her Nash about it.

John had his last will noted down in great haste by our son-in-law and the same day my dear was deceased:

*'Imprimis I give unto my wife my house in London.*
*Item I give unto my daughter Nash my house in Acton.*
*Item I give unto my daughter Nash my Meadow.*
*Item I give my goods and moneys unto my wife and my daughter Nash to be equally divided betwixt them.*
*Item concerning my study of Books, I leave them (said he) to you, my son Nash, to dispose of them as you see good.*
*As for my manuscripts, I would have given them to Master Boles if he had been here; but for as much as he is not here present, you may (son Nash) burn them or else do with them what you please.*

*Witnesses here unto Thomas Nashe, Simon Trappe.'*

How weird it is, such a testament, as if someone else speaks to you. No, we will not let his medical notes go up in smoke. How could we? His entire life's work, his heart and soul are in them. The herb jars and mortars - I just took them one by one in my hands and put them away. Precious objects with their beautiful glaze and colors. In the evening I often looked at them, when the apothecaries were off. And how carefully I have dusted them time and again. As long as your tools are in order and your wits quick, Hall would have said.

I felt secretly proud to have a practice at home. But for pride one must immediately ask forgiveness. Humility is everything and that is to your credit. But just a little bit of pride feels so good and strong. And proud I also had to be to distinguish between the poseurs and the people in need, between the braggarts and the modest brave people, between the sensationalists and the seriously sick.

How composed you always tried to be, Hall. You knew who you were dealing with. And with me the nuances of your feelings counted for something. I could tell whether you were concerned or relaxed, irritated or angry. One look at each other was enough, remember. We have been a nice team together, how well we understood one another. How much we loved each other. Sometimes we couldn't even grasp how much. 'For better - for worse. Till death do us part...'

I hope the rosemary will survive the winter - the herb of remembrance, friendship and fidelity. On our wedding day my friends presented you with a bunch of it, my groom. It was, as usual, tied up with golden silk and lace.

How often did you use the sweet herb in your prescriptions. It worked both inside and on the outside, as ointment or oil for skin and hair. It is good against loss of memory, nervousness and also a bit against melancholy. At Christmas we so often decorated the tables with it.

In spring, and sometimes again in August, I will cull every year as much as I can. I will for the rest of my life scent our home with it. And on top of that I will strew next summer a thousand petals of the early red rose, as a symbol for our wedding day and our deepest feelings for each other. Then I will, with all the love that is in me, live up to your most beautiful family device, darling:

## *'Remember and Forget Not.'*

# POSTSCRIPT

Susanna Shakespeare Hall would outlive her husband by fourteen years. She died on July the eleventh 1649, at sixty-six years of age. Five days later she was buried next to her husband, close by Shakespeare, in Holy Trinity Church. On Hall's tombstone the following was added in Latin:

*'Lest aught should be wanting to his tomb, his very faithful wife is at hand, and the companion of his life he has now also in death.'*

A few years after the death of her husband Susanna sold his patients' case notes to doctor James Cooke. This doctor was near Stratford with the Parliamentary troops stationed there, who opposed the Royalists at the time of the 'Civil War'. At the urging of a member of the family, he decided to call in to see Susanna and ask her whether she still had her husband's reports and whether he could see them. Susanna took out two manuscripts in Latin by Hall.

The story goes that she did not recognize his handwriting right away in one of these and that she at the insistence of Cooke responded in an irritated manner. It has been suggested that she herself might not have been able to read and write, and that she therefore did not recognize Hall's writings. *But* isn't it strange that she would not have recognized only one? And could it not be that Cooke insisted so on a sale that she thereby became irritated? While she hesitated whether she ought to part with something as unique as the lifework of her dearly beloved spouse, with such intimate details about the family too?!

However that may be, the precious *'Select Observations on English Bodies of Eminent Persons in desperate Diseases'* are preserved in this way through the translations of Doctor Cooke. He turned out to be especially impressed with the treatment of scurvy by his colleague, with which Hall was ahead of his time. Cooke was helped by one of the apothecaries of Hall, Court, to decipher the handwritten abbreviations in the prescriptions and treatments. The first edition was in 1657, the second in 1679 and the third in 1683. One original handwritten casebook in Latin by John Hall is in the British Library in London.

Eliza, the only child of John and Susanna Hall remained herself childless. She was widowed in 1647 and her Thomas Nash was buried on the fifth of April that year in the chancel of Trinity Church next to William Shakespeare. At his death Thomas Nash had allotted 'Nash's House' to his widow, but Shakespeare's New Place to another family member. Susanna and Elizabeth contested this successfully and got the house back.

On the thirtieth of January 1649, a shudder went through the country, when King Charles was beheaded in London. The King had been not very popular, but this was terribly cruel though and it was deeply believed that kings ruled according to the will of God. Charles I, however, had systematically ignored Parliament and his opponents had now assumed power. England became temporarily a Republic. The Civil War also ended up driving a wedge between Shakespeare's plays and public. In 1642 plays were banned and in 1647 entirely suppressed.

Eliza remarried on the fifth of June 1649, seemingly a tribute to the wedding day of her beloved parents and a month before the death of her mother. So her first marriage on the twenty second of April sixteen twenty six, precisely ten years after the death of her famous grandfather, definitely seems to be a tribute to the tenth anniversary of his death, and to his birthday. Sir John Barnard of Abington, a wealthy patron of the arts, who possessed a library, became her new husband. He had been a widower for the past six years with a family with eight children, four sons and four daughters, of whom at the time of his marriage with Eliza Hall she still had five under her care. In 1661 Barnard went on to obtain the title of 'baronet' for his merits as 'Royalist' during the Civil War, and so Eliza became Lady Barnard.

Presumably the spouses lived partly in New Place and partly in Abington Manor. Like Barnard, Eliza also was not without means. Her rich first husband, Thomas Nash, left her the house next to New Place, as well as his tithes in Shottery and any pastures that adjoined Clopton Bridge in Stratford. As the only surviving grandchild of Shakespeare - the sons Richard and Thomas of her aunt Judith died both already in 1639 - she was already wealthy and as sole heiress of her parents she also inherited a considerable amount of money and property from them.

Shakespeare's granddaughter would still live to see around 1660 that the theatres were allowed to open again. Then it was for the first time also possible for women to be an actress. England became a monarchy anew and Charles II ascended the throne. In Stratford the Puritans had preached in church for a considerable time, but now, during the Restoration, one could be open again to a more flexible view of the ministry.

Eliza died in 1670 at the age of sixty two in Abington and was buried there. She left to the descendants of her great aunt Joan Hart Shakespeare's house where he was born, the 'Birthplace' in Henley Street. Her husband Barnard obtained a lifelong usufruct of New Place. She had all her further property converted into money, so that she could leave a large part of it to the poorer relatives of her grandmother Anne Hathaway, of whom she named six in her will.

It was not possible to trace where exactly Eliza is buried in Abington. However, an American later saw to it that a memorial was erected there. Her husband died four years after her.

Susanna's sister Judith lived to be relatively old. February 1662 she died at the age of seventy seven. It is believed that Thomas Quiney died some ten years before her, in London during a visit to a brother of his.

With regard to the grave of Susanna Shakespeare: her bones are dug up and afterwards placed in the ossuary to make way for one Watts of Phyon Clifford. The inscription in Susanna's tombstone was erased on that occasion. This was restored in the year 1844 and the Watts-tombstone was placed next to those of the family Hall.

Susanna's epitaph describes how sensible and wise she was, and that something of Shakespeare was in her. Furthermore, that she knew how to comfort all and that her love and mercy will live on:

> '*Witty above her sex; but that's not all –*
> *Wise to Salvation was good Mistress Hall:*
> *Something of Shakespeare was in that, but this*
> *Wholly of Him with whom she's now in bliss.*
> *Then, passenger, hast ne'er a tear*
> *To weep with her that wept with all*
> *That wept, yet set herself to cheer*
> *Them up with comforts cordial?*
> *Her love shall live, her mercy spread,*
> *When thou hast ne'er a tear to shed.*'

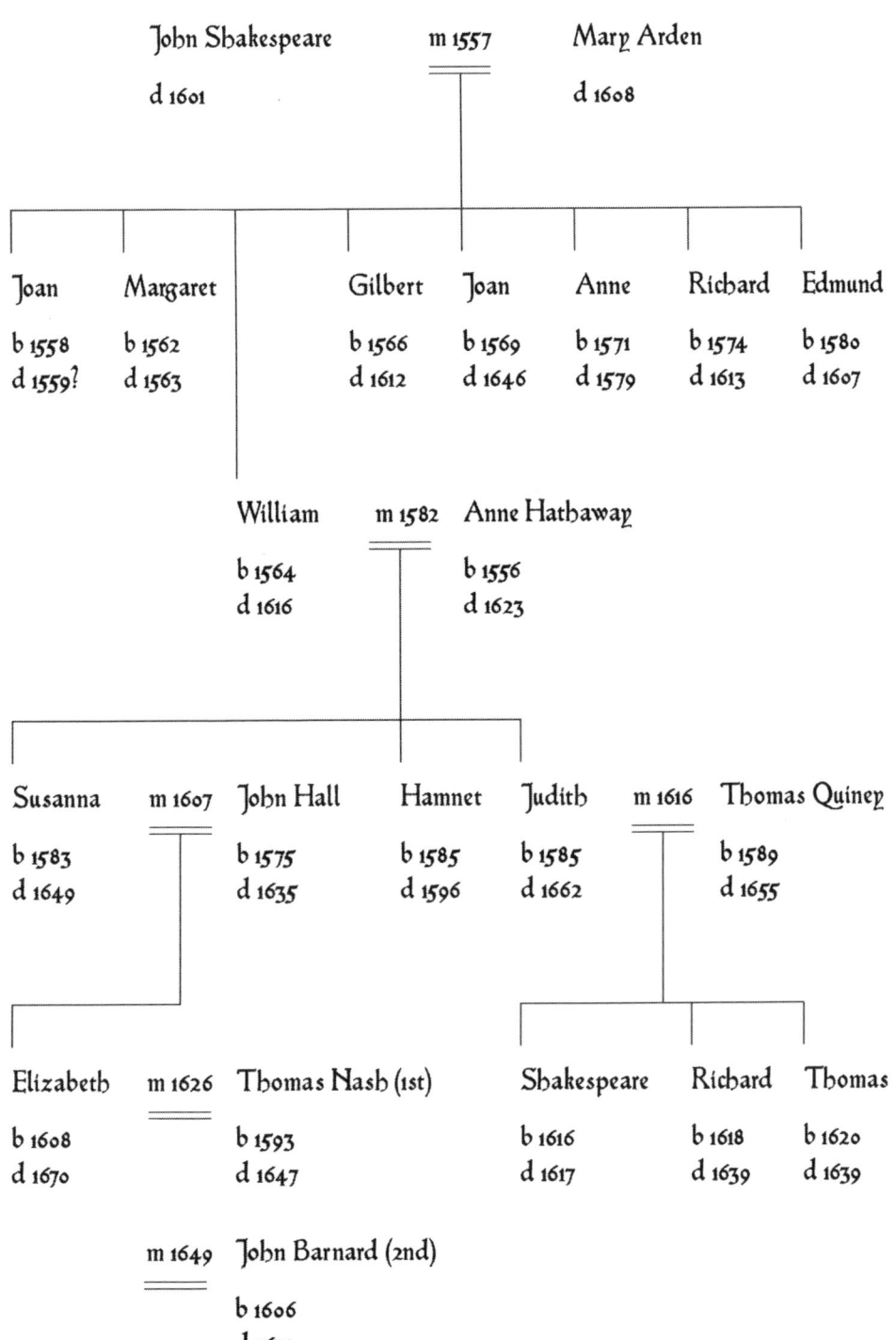

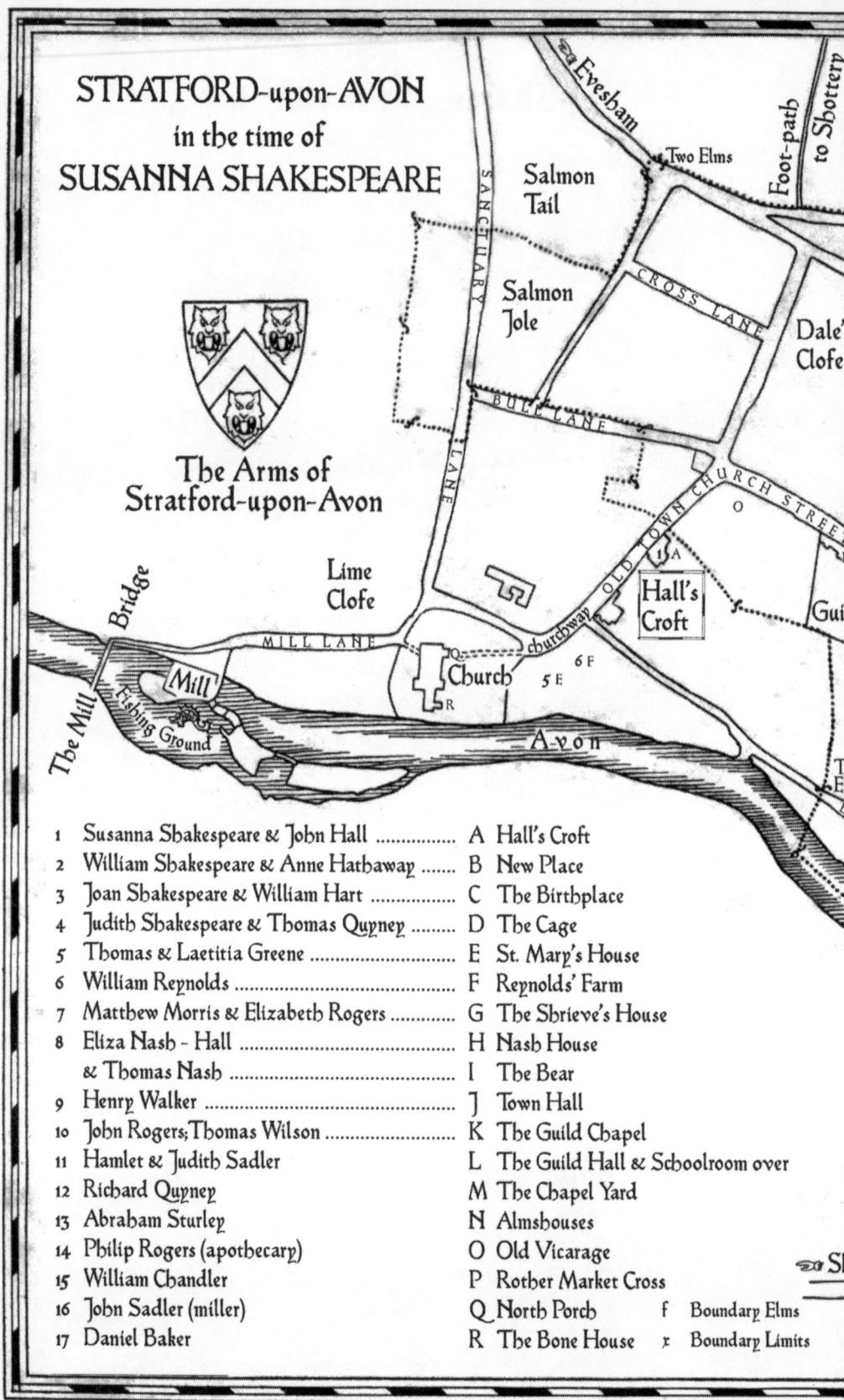

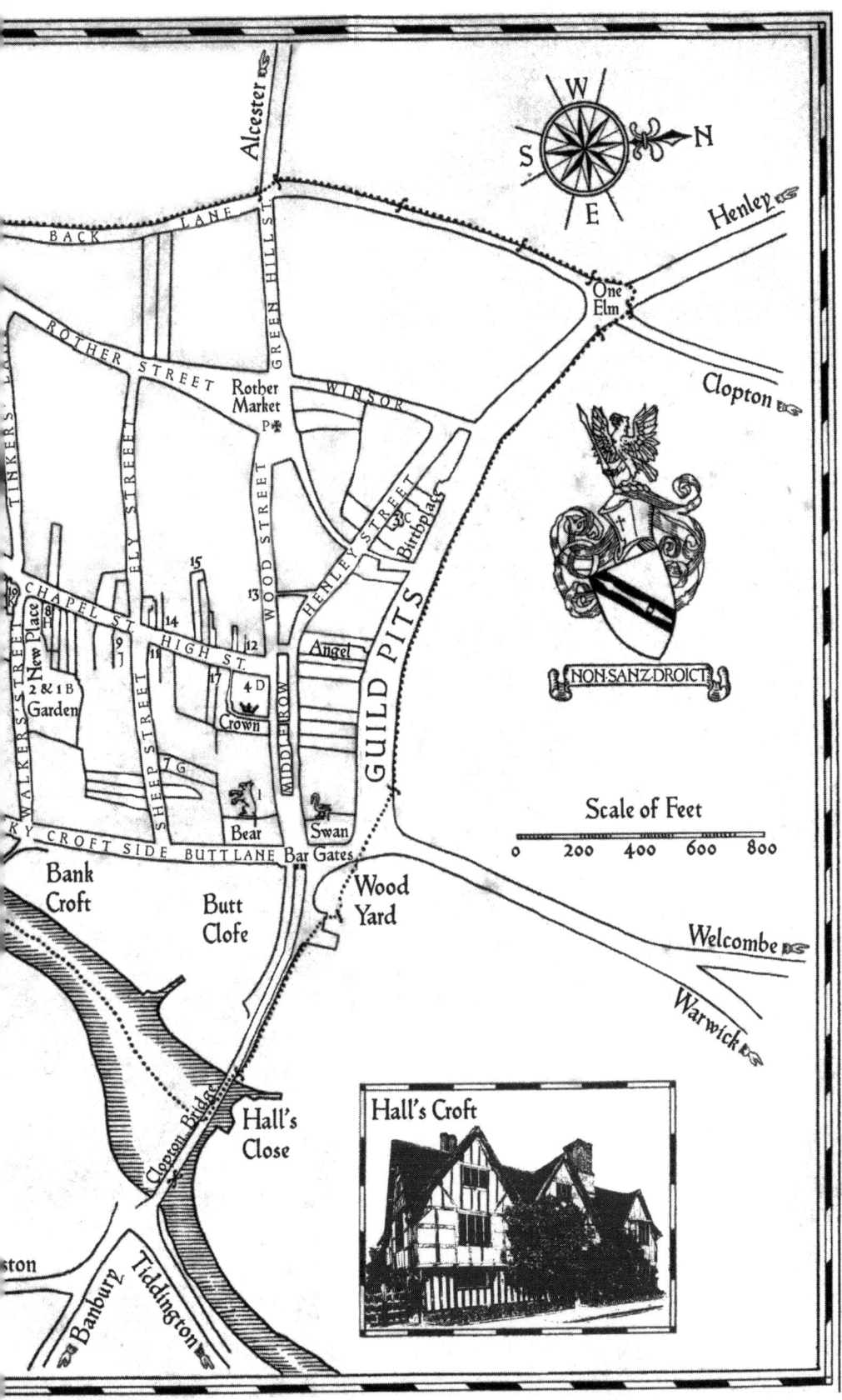

# ACKNOWLEDGEMENTS

I want to praise all guides and fellow workers of The Shakespeare Centre in Stratford-upon-Avon for their never ending effort to inform those interested in Shakespeare, as if the latter in all these years are the very first. Also I would like to pay tribute to their expertise, knowledge, courtesy and enthusiasm. This affects any visitor in all houses of the Shakespeare Birthplace Trust, including in the practice and home of Susanna and John, 'Hall's Croft', in Old Town Stratford.

I am also indebted to Mrs. C.M. Vaughan of 'Robert Vaughan, antiquarian booksellers' in Stratford-upon-Avon at the time, for the wonderful editions of the books of Edgar I. Fripp and many other Shakespeare books.

I especially like to thank my husband, for his help in the interpretation of medical affairs. Together we visited the Shakespeare-houses in Stratford and the countless performances of Shakespeare's plays at home and abroad with the greatest joy and enthusiasm. With him I thank our dearest children and grandchildren for their love, inspiration and patience during this writing process.

Last but not least I had the unconditional support of my late brother, my dear sisters (-in-law) and brothers-in-law, darling niece, nephews and their families, girlfriends, friends and England-loving neighbours.

Concerning the English edition I want to thank Anna George from Bristol, England, for her tremendous effort and support during the translation process. I couldn't have managed without her, her knowledge, kindness and patience.

Emma Mulveagh and colleagues from The Shakespeare Bookshop in Henley Street in Stratford-upon-Avon I like to thank for her kind mails and their enthusiasm for an English edition.

Publisher Perry Pierik and his staff, especially Sylvia Kamerbeek, from Aspekt Publishing I need to thank for giving me another chance to edit Susanna Shakespeare, now in English.

# QUOTES

The quotes from the works of Shakespeare are from STANLEY WELLS' WILLIAM SHAKESPEARE, The COMPLETE WORKS, 1988:

In chapter III: Quote with regard to Constance from King John, III iv, from Wells p. 412.
In chapter XVIII: quotes from The Tempest, IV i, from Wells p. 1184.
In chapter XXIV: quote from Cymbeline, IV ii, from Wells p. 1154.
In chapter XXV: quote from Shakespeare's Sonnet 145, from Wells p. 769.
In chapter XXV: quote from The Tempest (Prospero to Ariël), V i, from Wells p. 1189.
In chapter XXV: quote from the Epilogue of Prospero in The Tempest, from Wells p. 1189.


THE OTHER QUOTATIONS:
(With Fripp is meant: E.I. Fripp, Man & Artist, part II)
(The sayings from Hoes are translated in English by Alida Rijnders.)

Chapter VI : the testament of the old William Hall, from Marcham p. 20.
: the motto of John Hall (*rudder/oars*), from Lane p. xxviii.
: the words of thanks to the Lord God stand behind many cases of Hall.

Chapter VII: '*old Father Thames*', from Wood p. 301, at the illustration.
Chapter VIII: phrases from the Hippocratic Oath, from Hoes p. 22.

Chapter XI: idem + saying Hippocrates: '*life is short ...*', from Hoes, p. 15 + 35.
: saying Galenus: '*Trust and hope ...*', Hoes p. 49.
Chapter XV: quote from Richard Jones' book, from Sim, The Tudor Housewife p.6.
Chapter XVI: quotes from the diary of Thomas Greene, from Fripp p. 806 - 809.
Chapter XVII: from Shakespeare's will: '*in perfect health and memory*', from Fripp p.821.
: data on Shakespeare's will and the marriage of Judith, according to Fripp 821-826.
Chapter XVIII: text on the tomb of Shakespeare: '*Good Friend ...*', from Fripp p. 829.
: '*Ad Febrem Purpuream*', from Lane p. xxii.
Chapter XXI: '*Hang him, kill him...*', from Fripp p. 839.
Chapter XXII: quotes from 'King's Book of Sports', from Fripp p. 839-842.
: quotes from the bill in Chancery: '*malicious,... behaviour*', from Fripp p.841-842.
: quote: '*that Master Rogers ... Chamberlain*', from Fripp p. 844-5.
Chapter XXIII: quote from the will of the old William Hall: '*have ... things*', from Mitchell p.7.
Chapter XXIV: quote on grave Anne Hathaway: '*Ubera, tu mater ...* ', from Fripp p. 854 + idem note 1.
Chapter XXV: quotes Ben Jonson with regard to Shakespeare, from Wells, The Complete Works, p. xlv/xlvi.
Chapter XXIX: from the Stratford minutes: '*Jo[hannes] Hall...... a[bsens],*' & '*Master Hall.... Serjeants*', from Fripp p. 886/887.
: letter of Sid Davenport, from Lane p. xxvi/xxvii and Joseph p. 27/28/29 .

Chapter XXX: quote from Hall: *'Health is from the* Lord.*'* from Lane: Observation I, facing p. 1.
: quotes about illness doctor Hall himself, from Lane p. 298-301: Observ. LX.

Chapter XXXI: quote from Bishop: *'That the said Master Hall...'*, from Mitchell p. 104.
: quote from Stratford minutes: *'acrimonious and quarrelsome'* from Mitchell p. 103.

Chapter XXXII: quote from Thomas Quiney: *'Blessed is the man...'* from Fripp p. 887.

Chapter XXXIV: epitaph of John Hall: *'Hall is laid here,...on all.'* from Fripp p. 891 and idem note 5.
: Testament Hall: *'Imprimis I give unto...'* from Fripp p. 891.
: Motto of Hall: *'Remember...'*, from Mitchell, below illustration opposite p. 86.

Postscript: The lines about Susanna on Hall's grave: *'Lest aught...'* from Fripp p. 905, note 1.
: lines from epitaph of Susanna: *'Witty above...'*, from Fripp p. 905.

# IMPORTANT SOURCES

FRIPP, Edgar I.: *SHAKESPEARE, MAN & ARTIST*, Volume II; Oxford University Press/Humphrey Milford, London, 1938

FRIPP, Edgar I.: *Shakespeare's STRATFORD*, Oxford University Press/Humphrey Milford, London, 1928

JOSEPH, Harriet: *Shakespeare's Son-in-law, JOHN HALL, Man and Physician*, Printed in the United States of America (sic), fourth printing, 1993

LANE, Joan: *JOHN HALL and his Patients, The Medical Practice of Shakespeare's Son-in-Law*, Medical Commentary by Melvin Earles, The Shakespeare Birthplace Trust/The Shakespeare Centre, Stratford-upon-Avon, 1996

MITCHELL, C. Martin: *The SHAKESPEARE CIRCLE*, Cornish Brothers Ltd., Birmingham, 1947

WELLS, Stanley and Taylor, Gary: *WILLIAM SHAKESPEARE, The COMPLETE WORKS*, compact ed., Clarendon Press, Oxford, 1988

# LITERARY REFERENCES

AKROYD, Peter: *SHAKESPEARE, De Biografie [ SHAKESPEARE, The Biography (in Dutch)]*, in Dutch translation by Erik Bindervoet and Robbert-Jan Henkes)], Meulenhoff, Amsterdam, 2006

BACHRACH, Prof. Dr. A.G.H. and others: *RONDOM SHAKESPEARE [ Around Shakespeare (in Dutch)]* , W. de Haan N.V., Zeist / Antwerp, 1964

BANGS, Jeremy Dupertuis: *STRANGERS and PILGRIMS, Travellers and Sojourners*, General Society of Mayflower Descendants, Plymouth, 2009

BATE, Jonathan: *The GENIUS of SHAKESPEARE,* Picador, London, 1997

BEARMAN, Robert: *SHAKESPEARE in the Stratford Records*, in association with the Shakespeare Birthplace Trust & the Shakespeare Centre – Stratford-upon-Avon, Alan Sutton Publ. Ltd. Redwood Books, Trowbridge, Wiltshire, 1994

BEARMAN, Robert: *THE HISTORY of an ENGLISH BOROUGH, STRATFORD-UPON-AVON 1196-1996,* Sutton Publishing Ltd./The Shakespeare Birthplace Trust, Gloucestershire/Stratford-upon-Avon, 1997

BOYCE, Charles: *SHAKESPEARE A – Z*, Roundtable Press, New York, 1991

BRADBROOK M.C.: *SHAKESPEARE, The poet in his world*, Univ. Press, Cambridge, 1978

Dr. L.A.J. BURGERSDIJK: *De COMPLETE WERKEN van WILLIAM SHAKESPEARE [The COMPLETE WORKS of WILLIAM SHAKESPEARE (in Dutch)]*, in drie delen [in three parts], Sijthoff's ed. N.V., Leiden, 1941

BUSSAGLI, Marco: *Het MENSELIJK LICHAAM [the HUMAN BODY (in Dutch)]*, Ludion, Gent, 2007

CHANCELLOR PRESS: *The illustrated Stratford SHAKESPEARE*, Reed Consumer Books Ltd., London-Toronto, 1993

CHUTE, Marchette: *SHAKESPEARE OF LONDON*, Secker & Warburg, London, 1951

COOK, Judith: *WOMEN IN SHAKESPEARE*, Virgin Books, London, 1990

CULPEPER, Nicholas: *CULPEPER'S COMPLETE HERBAL*, Arcturus Publishing, Singapore, 2009

DAVIDSON, Caroline: *A WOMAN'S WORK IS NEVER DONE*, Chatto & Windus Ltd., London, 1982

DODD, A.H.: *ELIZABETHAN ENGLAND*, Book Club Associates, London, 1973

DOVER WILSON, John: *The Essential SHAKESPEARE*, Cambridge University Press, Cambridge 1962

DUBY, Georges & Michell Perrot: *GESCHIEDENIS van de VROUW, van Renaissance tot de moderne tijd [WOMEN'S HISTORY, from the Renaissance to modern times (in Dutch)]*, Agon BV, Amsterdam, 1992

DUBY, Georges & Philippe Ariès: *GESCHIEDENIS van het PERSOONLIJK LEVEN [HISTORY of PERSONAL LIFE (in Dutch)]*, Agon BV, Amsterdam, 1993

DUSINBERRE, Juliet: *SHAKESPEARE and the Nature of Women*, The Macmillan Press Ltd., London & Basingstoke, 1975

ECCLES, Mark: *SHAKESPEARE in WARWICKSHIRE*, The University of Wisconsin Press, Madison, USA, 1961

EDWARDS, Anne-Marie: *Walking with WILLIAM SHAKESPEARE*, Jones Books, Madison Wisconsin, USA, 2005

ELTON, Charles Isaac and Hamilton Thompson, A.: *WILLIAM SHAKESPEARE, His Family and Friends*, John Murray, London, 1904

FRASER, Russell: *SHAKESPEARE, THE LATER YEARS*, Columbia University Press, New York, 1992

FRIPP, Edgar I.: *SHAKESPEARE, MAN & ARTIST*, Volume I, Oxford University Press/Humphrey Milford, London, 1938

FRIPP, Edgar I.: *SHAKESPEARE'S HAUNTS near Stratford*, Oxford University Press, London, 1929

FRIPP, Edgar I.: *SHAKESPEARE STUDIES*, Oxford University Press, London, 1930

FROUD, Brian & Alan Lee: *DE ELFEN [FAERIES (in Dutch)]*, Dutch Transl. by C.J. van Tilborch and Ernst van Altena, Van Holkema & Warendorf / Unieboek bv, Bussum, 1979

GRAY, Arthur: *SHAKESPEARE'S SON-IN-LAW*, Ohio State University, W. Heffer & sons Ltd., Cambridge, 1939

GRAY, J.W.: *SHAKESPEARE'S Marriage and Departure from Stratford*, Chapman & Hall L.D., London, 1905

GREENBLATT, Stephan: *WILLIAM en de WERELD [WILLIAM and the WORLD (in Dutch)]*, in Dutch translation by Marijke Koch and Albert Witteveen, De Bezige Bij, Amsterdam, 2004

GREER, Germaine: *SHAKESPEARE'S WIFE*, Bloomsbury Publishing, London, 2007

HALLIDAY, F.E.: *The Life of SHAKESPEARE*, Gerald Duckworth & co, London, 1964

HALLIDAY, F.E.: *SHAKESPEARE, biografie in woord en beeld [ SHAKESPEARE, biography in word and pictures (in Dutch)]*, Kruseman, Den Haag [the Hague], 1963

HOES, M.J.A.J.M.: *HISTORIOGRAFIE , Capita over soma en psyche vanaf de oudheid [HISTORIOGRAPHY, Capita about soma and psyche from antiquity (in Dutch)]*, Ciba-Geigy BV/Words & Pages BV, Arnhem, 1995

HONAN, Park: *SHAKESPEARE, A LIFE*, Oxford University Press, New York, 1998

JONES, Jeanne: *FAMILY LIFE IN SHAKESPEARE'S ENGLAND Stratford-upon-Avon 1570 – 1630*, Sutton publishing, the Shakespeare Birthplace Trust, Stratford-upon-Avon, 1996

KERR, Jessica: *SHAKESPEARE'S FLOWERS*, illustrated by Anne Ophelia Dowden, Longmans Young Books Ltd., London, no date

KOTT, Jan: *SHAKESPEARE Our Contemporary*, Routledge, London, 1988

LEE, Stephen J.: *The REIGN OF ELIZABETH I, 1558-1603*, Routledge, London & New York, 2007

LYONS, Albert S., M.D. & R. Joseph Petrucelli, II, M.D.: *MEDICINE, An illustrated History*, Abradale Press, Harry N. Abrams Publ., New York, 1978

MARCHAM, Frank: *WILLIAM SHAKESPEARE AND HIS FAMILY, WILLIAM SHAKESPEARE AND HIS DAUGHTER SUSANNAH*, Grafton & Co., London, 1931

MUIR, Kenneth: *LAST PERIODS of SHAKESPEARE, RACINE AND IBSEN*, Liverpool Univ. Press, Liverpool, 1961

MUIR, Kenneth & Schoenbaum, S.: *A New Companion to SHAKESPEARE STUDIES*, Cambridge University Press, Cambridge, 1979

PODLECH, Dieter: *HERBS and HEALING PLANTS of BRITAIN & EUROPE*, Harper Collins, London, 2008

PRITCHARD, R.E.: *SHAKESPEARE'S ENGLAND*, Sutton Publ., Gloucestershire, 2006

ROWSE, A.L.: *The ENGLAND of ELIZABETH*, Macmillan & co. Ltd., London, 1951

ROWSE, A.L.: *WILLIAM SHAKESPEARE, a biography*, Macmillan & co., London, 1963

SCHOENBAUM, S.: *WILLIAM SHAKESPEARE, A compact documentary life*, Oxford Univ. Press, New York, 1978

SEEL, Graham E. and Smith, David L.: *The EARLY STUART KINGS, 1603-1642*, Routledge, London and New York, 2001

SEITZ, Paul: *HET COMPLETE KRUIDENHANDBOEK [The COMPLETE HERBAL HANDBOOK (in Dutch)]*, Deltas, Zuid-Nederlandse uitg. NV [Southern-Dutch ed. NV], Aartselaar, Belgium, 2010

SIM, Alison: *FOOD & FEAST IN TUDOR ENGLAND*, Sutton Publishing, Phoenix Mill, Stroud, 2005

SIM, Alison: *MASTERS AND SERVANTS IN TUDOR ENGLAND*, Sutton Publishing, Phoenix Mill, Stroud, 2006

SIM, Alison: *PLEASURES AND PASTIMES IN TUDOR ENGLAND*, The History Press, The Mill, Stroud, 2009

SIM, Alison: *THE TUDOR HOUSE WIFE*, Sutton Publishing, Stroud, 1996

STEELE, Philip: *TUDORS, STUARTS & CIVIL WAR*, Miles Kelly Publishing Ltd., Great Bardfield, Essex, 2002

STOPES, C. C.: *SHAKESPEARE'S FAMILY*, Elliot Stock, London, 1901

SUTHERLAND, James, and Hurstfield, Joel: *SHAKESPEARE'S WORLD*, Edward Arnold Publishers Ltd., London, 1964

WELLS, Stanley: *The CAMBRIDGE COMPANION to SHAKESPEARE STUDIES*, Cambridge University Press, Cambridge, 1986

WELLS, Stanley: *SHAKESPEARE FOR ALL TIME*, Oxford Univ. Press, New York, 2003

WILSON, J.D.: *LIFE IN SHAKESPEARE'S ENGLAND*, Cambridge University Press, Cambridge, 1949

WOOD, Michael: *IN SEARCH OF SHAKESPEARE*, BBC, Worldwide Ltd., London, 2003

WOODS, Nicola: *KRUIDEN en SPECERIJEN [Collins Gem Herbs and Spices (in Dutch)]*, Spectrum, Utrecht, 2003 (Winkler Prins MINI)

WOOLEY, Benjamin: *THE HERBALIST, Nicholas Culpeper and the fight for medical freedom*, Harper Perennial, London, 2005